The Chronicles of Music Majors

Ashley Rescot

Rescot Creative Publishing
Springfield, Illinois

The Chronicles of Music Majors

ISBN 978-1-7366044-0-3 paperbook
ISBN 978-1-7366044-1-0 eBook
ISBN 978-1-7366044-2-7 audiobook
© 2021 Ashley Rescot

All rights reserved. No part of this publication may be reproduced, distributed, or transmitted in any form or by any means, including photocopying, recording, or other electronic or mechanical methods, without the prior written permission of the publisher, except in the case of brief quotations embodied in critical reviews and certain other noncommercial uses permitted by copyright law. For permission requests, please use the contact form found on www.rescotcreative.com

This is a work of fiction. Names, characters, businesses, events and incidents are the products of the author's imagination. Any resemblance to actual persons, living or deceased, or actual events is purely coincidental.

Cover Design:
Heather Deiter
Interior Design:
Robert Rescot

Library of Congress Control Number: 2021937249
Rescot, Ashley
Chronicles of Music Majors / Ashley Rescot 1st ed.

First Edition

Praise for

The Chronicles of Music Majors

Ashley Rescot jazzes up the lives of music students in ways that are both fun and easy to relate to. Whether or not you are a musician, you will enjoy learning about music and romance from this charming collection of characters.

-Dr. Robin Wallace

Professor of Musicology, Baylor University
Author of: *Hearing Beethoven: A Story of Musical Loss and Discovery*

The Chronicles of Music Majors is a rollicking good time! I found myself on the edge of my seat, perpetually enticed to read "just one more page". Ashley Rescot's artful depictions of the inner workings of Belton University's School of Music left me longing for my music major days. A true gift to music lovers of every age, and a delightful read from start to finish!

-Dr. Chelsea Dark

Horn player
Licensed Psychologist,
www.austinsleeppsychologist.com

Ashley Rescot's The Chronicles of Music Majors *offers readers a refreshing lift as she invites us into her fictional music world. Her sweet romantic stories hit all the right notes with perfect pitch. My favorite story would have to be the last one I read–seriously, it was hard to choose because each has its own unique twist. A delicious read. If you have a musical background or simply love music, this collection of stories is a must.*

-Mary Pat Johns

Author of faith-filled stories of hope and redemption,
Contributor to *Chicken Soup for the Soul* series
www.marypatjohns.com

As a lifelong singer and professional performer I loved Ashley Rescot's short story series The Chronicles of Music Majors. Her descriptive writing style and interesting characters pulled me in completely. In fact, I was disappointed when the story was over! I wanted more! I especially loved the short stories "Christmas Glee Club" and "Get a Händel on It." These two stories in particular should be fondly reminiscent to anyone who has ever participated in a high school chorus or orchestra concert.

-Charleen Ayers

Adjunct Professor of Voice, Friends University
Opera and Musical Theatre Performer

My mother was a music teacher, and Ashley's characters brought to life so many memories of that special time in my childhood. Her vivid descriptions bloomed the aroma of leather-covered violin cases, the tinkling of piano keys, the om-pa-pa of accordion notes, and the excitement that filled the concert halls. As I turned the pages, I wore the shoes of the students at the fictional Belton University and wished the story would never end.

-Amre Cortadino

Author, 2020 1st place ACFW Virginia Crown Award Winner, Suspense, 2019 Finalist ACFW Genesis Contest, www.merryheartink.com

I really enjoyed reading these stories! So many experiences that are universal to college-aged students, discovering life and love in the midst of their musical studies. Each one strikes the balance of developing the characters and situations within the structural confines of a short story. Well done!

-Devon Carpenter

Harpist
Teacher / Owner
The Music Factory
www.springfieldmusicfactory.com

Table of Contents

Resources

To enhance your reading of this book, the author has assembled additional supporting resources, including:

- audio playlists to share the music referenced in the book,
- digital Belton University book club on social media to connect with other fans,
- Questions for Reflection for educators or book clubs, (also found at the end of this book), and
- an opportunity to connect directly with the author.

All of these resources and more can be found on the author's website at: www.rescotcreative.com (or scan the QR code below).

Preface

When I was two years old, my mother placed a tiny box violin in my hands. Ever since that time, music has played a pivotal role in my life. I'm always fascinated by the correlation between music and literature, and for me the lines often blur together like the colors in an impressionist painting.

After teaching for nearly two decades, I have noticed that music students respond well to stories. As a result, I wanted to create a fictional university for them where characters explore the world of music, delving into music history, composition, and concerts, all while discovering love and friendship along the way. My hope is to inspire the next generation of musicians, encourage current music professionals, and share my love of the art with non-musicians.

This collection of short stories can be read in any order, all at once, or broken up over a series of months. For teachers interested in using them with their young adult classes or studios, the stories include several seasonal themes, as well as a variety of instruments. Feel free to select the ones that appeal most to your students. Don't forget to check out the musical playlists that accompany the narratives on my website.

If you enjoy this collection, I would greatly appreciate if you could leave a review on your book retailer's website. This helps others discover the series and allows me to continue writing music fiction!

Acknowledgments

With this publication of my first book, I want to acknowledge many of the people who have encouraged me in my own creative journey.

To my husband, Robert, for giving me a real-life romance, for his tireless support of my music and writing, and for helping me every step of the way in navigating my new role as an author.

To my mother, Allison, who first taught me to play the violin and then how to teach.

To my father and grandparents, who came to countless recitals and supported me as my biggest fans.

To my parents-in-law, for loving and supporting me in my career like a daughter.

To my music teachers, including my aunts, piano teachers, voice instructors, and college professors, without whom I wouldn't be the musician and writer I am today.

To my students and their families, for being a joy to teach.

To my wonderful editor, Leslie L. McKee, fellow musician and phenomenal writer, for her dedication to the craft and encouraging words.

To my cover designer, my cousin Heather Deiter, for her amazing ability to visualize my vision for the book.

To my Uncle Brent, for his diligence in proofreading my stories to make them shine.

To my dear critique partners in ACFW, for their expertise and support in helping these stories come to life.

To my fellow writers and coach Kent Sanders in The Daily Writer Community, for their accountability and encouragement in all aspects of the writing career.

To my Creator, the One who gives people the gift of creativity, as we were fashioned in His image.

I could not have accomplished this without
all of your support!

This book is dedicated to my mother, Allison,
my first music teacher.

A Change in the Winds

A Back-to-School Story

Brandon clamped his large fingers around the thick neck of his six-foot upright bass. He glanced over his shoulder at the clock on the back wall of the concert hall. *Will this rehearsal ever end?* Still twenty minutes until break. He sighed.

The conductor, a man in his mid-thirties dressed in a crisp button-down shirt, waved his arms in perfect precision in front of the violin section. As always, the violinists sped through exciting melodies while Brandon plunked out repetitive bass lines. *That's what happens when you choose bass in junior high orchestra.*

At that time in his life, he'd wanted a hobby to keep him away from home as long as possible. His twelve-year-old self never would have dreamed he'd end up a music major at Belton University. A relaxed, go-with-the-flow guy, he'd never fully identified with the "ork dorks" in other sections of the orchestra. Yet seven years later, here he sat, perched on a stool on a fancy stage, a sophomore in college.

Brandon glanced at the score in front of him. Several measures of rests spanned the page. He set his bow on the music stand and ran one hand through his shaggy brown hair. The third movement of Dvorak's Eighth Symphony filled his ears. The nineteenth-century composer possessed a knack for beautiful melodic lines. If only he'd shared more of them with the lower strings.

After the movement wound to a close, the conductor wiped his forehead and gestured to the brass section. Brandon jerked to attention as trumpet blasts pierced the air. No chance to doze during this movement. He squinted at the notes on the page. Dvorak had finally given the melody to the low strings. Time to focus.

His instrument sang as he slid his bow over the strings. When the music's intensity rose, Brandon increased the pressure on the bow. How exhilarating! He pulled his last stroke through with a flourish.

He slumped lower on the stool. A new sound jolted him back to attention—this time not trumpet blasts, but the sweet song of a flute. His gaze moved to the woodwinds. A thrill of excitement rippled down his spine. A slender girl with wavy brunette hair held a flute to her rosy lips. Chestnut eyes gleamed behind small glasses perched on her perky nose.

Brandon swallowed. As stunning as the music she played, the flutist's solo soared over the orchestra like a bird above the midwestern plains. How had he never noticed her before? And how could he attract her attention?

###

Francesca caught a quick breath between phrases. This flute solo demanded every ounce of breath support she possessed. After playing in the Belton University Wind Ensemble for the past two years, she'd finally achieved her dream—acceptance into the Belton Symphony Orchestra, as a junior.

Her fingers flew over the slender silver metal as if on autopilot. She'd played this solo countless times in the practice room but never with an orchestra.

At the age of nine she'd joined the school band and loved every minute of it. She'd sat first flute all through high school, so her decision to major in music was no surprise.

After the last note of her solo died away, she lowered the instrument to her lap and wet her dry lips. She glanced at the clock at the back of the concert hall. Almost time for break. Her gaze dropped to the bassist in front of the clock. With large, muscular arms wrapped around his instrument, he resembled a teddy bear hugging a giant violin. The bass suited him in size. *Cute.* Her heartbeat quickened. How had she never noticed this guy? She'd have remembered that tan complexion and mischievous smile.

The conductor rapped on his music stand. "Take five. After the break, we'll run the last movement again." He shuffled the music in front of him, then strode off stage.

"Nice job."

Francesca turned to face Carl, the clarinetist seated behind her, his instrument in hand. A senior now, he'd joined the symphony a year ago. He pointed to her flute. "Not an easy part."

She shook her head. "My fingers were shaking."

He laughed. "It gets easier over time. You need to relax."

A tense smile pulled at the corners of her mouth. "How?"

He cocked his head to the side. "I'll think of something. Right now, I need to catch up with Brandon."

"Who?"

"A buddy of mine." He sauntered away.

Francesca turned back to her music. Five minutes to practice before rehearsal resumed.

After the short break, the conductor raised his arms, baton in hand. The trumpet fanfare rang in Francesca's ears as if to rouse her to action. The muscles in her fingers clamped the instrument.

When the low strings took over the melody, her gaze moved to the bass section in search of the cute teddy bear. He wasn't there. *Don't be stupid, Francesca. You don't even know him. Focus.*

She raised her flute and drew a deep breath.

As she placed the metal to her lips, a loud honk jolted her out of position. *What on earth is Carl up to?*

She twisted to flash him a fierce glare. But it wasn't Carl.

"What?" Her fingers tightened on the flute.

The teddy bear bassist sat in the chair behind her, Carl's clarinet clutched in his massive hand. He grinned.

Her stomach lurched. Where was Carl?

Out of the corner of her eye, she glimpsed a wave from the bass section. Sure enough, Carl sat on a stool, dwarfed behind the enormous instrument.

Warmth crept into her cheeks as she resumed her solo, all nerves with the cute guy behind her.

The conductor shot daggers from his eyes as he surveyed the orchestra in search of the troublemaker.

After her solo, Francesca spun around to face the bass player. "What in the world?"

He extended his hand. "Hi there. Nice to meet you. I'm Brandon."

She hesitated, then shook it. Electricity shot through her arm. "Why on earth did you trade instruments?"

Brandon chuckled and scratched his stubbled chin. "Carl said you needed a change in the winds."

Francesca pursed her lips. "And you agreed? You're in a heap of trouble."

He winked. "It's all right. I've got the best seat in the house."

###

The following night, Francesca slipped into a blue dress and matching heels. How had she allowed that smooth-talking bass player to convince her to go on a date with him the night before their big concert? What a schmoozer. If only the butterflies in her stomach would settle down.

She peaked at herself in the mirror and ran a hand through her hair to smooth it. Why did she care what this guy, Brandon, thought anyway?

Knock, knock. She opened the door to find Brandon leaning against the wall, a bouquet of lilies in hand.

A large grin spread across his face as he handed them to her. “For you.”

She held the flowers to her nose and inhaled the glorious fragrance. How had he known lilies were her favorite flower? Maybe Carl had told him after she’d gushed about them last spring. The two guys appeared quite chummy at rehearsal.

Brandon looped his thumbs into his khaki pockets. “Where do you wanna go for dinner? I hear the new Italian place is good.”

“Antonio’s? Yes, it’s fabulous. I ought to know, since I’m Italian.”

He chuckled. “I figured, based on your name. I love Italian food.”

“Maybe I could whip something up for you sometime.” The words were out before she could stop them. She’d assumed they’d make it to a second date. What if tonight was a fiasco?

"I'm sure you're a great cook. And I'd be happy to help. I make killer garlic bread out of a box." He winked.

"All right. I'll put you on garlic bread duty." Maybe this wouldn't turn out too bad after all.

A few minutes later, they arrived at the restaurant. At dinner, they split an order of Italian salad, spaghetti, and manicotti, Francesca's favorite.

She gestured at the tube-shaped pasta on the plate, one drenched in marinara, the other in a creamy Alfredo sauce. "I used to make these all the time with my mother."

Brandon cut off a piece and forked it into his mouth. "Really good. I bet you had fun cooking with your Mom. Mine was always too busy to bother teaching me how to cook—thought it was a waste of time."

Francesca scooped a bite of the pasta into her mouth. The creamy goodness filled her from the inside out with food and fond memories. "Why did she consider cooking a waste of time?"

He shrugged. "I dunno. Didn't like the extra mess, I suppose."

Without thinking, she reached across the table and placed her hand on his. "I wouldn't think it a waste of time. I'll teach you to cook any day."

A shiver tingled up her arm as he laced his fingers in hers. "I'm glad to know someone cares about my culinary advancement." His eyes twinkled.

###

The next day, Brandon straightened the bow tie on his tux between movements of the Dvorak Symphony. Francesca's big solo was coming up, and he hoped she'd nail it. Guilt pricked his conscience. He'd kept her out too late the previous night. Not intentionally, but they'd had so much to talk about he'd lost track of the time. He should have known better than to keep the star flute player out the night before her concert.

His eyes darted in her direction. *Wow!* She looked dazzling in a little black dress. Maybe she'd wear it on their next date, if she agreed to one.

Seconds later, the sound of the flute filled the concert hall. Her puckered mouth kissed the metal as her fingers flew over the instrument. What he wouldn't give to kiss her right now.

The audience erupted with applause at the end of the Symphony. The conductor gestured at Francesca to encourage her to stand. She flashed a smile at the audience, then glanced his way. His heartbeat quickened. Maybe she was thinking about him after all.

As he tucked his bass safely inside its gargantuan case after the concert, a hand pressed against his shoulder.

"Francesca." His breath caught in his throat. "You were wonderful. I was worried—"

She popped a piece of a delicious pastry into his mouth.

The chocolate melted on his tongue. "This is amazing. What is it?"

"A cannoli." She handed him a box of the tiny desserts.

He smiled. "Thanks. They look like miniature flutes."

"I think that's why I love them so much." She pulled one out and held it to her lips like her instrument. *Those gorgeous pink lips.* "Do you want to learn how to make them?"

His mouth went dry. He cleared his throat. "Yeah."

She beamed. "Good. It's a date."

Yes, a second date. In spite of the reprimand he'd received from the conductor, this change in the winds had turned out well after all.

“Bach” from the Grave

A Halloween Story

Adam Heckel twisted his hands in his lap and shifted himself on the lumpy couch in the music school's locker room. A freshman at Belton University, he'd pledged the band fraternity, Beta Alpha Nu Delta. At least the hazing hadn't been too bad so far. Nothing compared to other fraternities. Sure, he'd stayed up all night cleaning after the frat party a couple of nights ago. And the older guys had forced the pledges to sing in polka dot boxers outside the girls' dorm at three in the morning. But at least no one had shoved his head in a toilet like in high school. Yet.

"Heckel. Get over here." Barry, the senior trombonist, waved one large arm, gesturing for Adam to join him next to the lockers.

A twinge of terror passed through Adam's body as he strode next to the guy. The metal bars on the instrument lockers brought back uncomfortable memories from high school. Playing the bassoon hadn't been an easy choice, especially when the other kids found out the unfortunate Spanish translation of the word. After that discovery, they'd stuffed him in a locker on a regular basis.

Barry crossed his arms. "So what do you think?"

"Um, about what?" Adam's voice squeaked.

"About the Fraternity Fall Festival. It's up to you pledges to decide what to do."

Adam swallowed. "How about a chili cookoff?"

"No good." Barry scowled. "The Fijis do that every year."

"Maybe a haunted house?"

"Are you an idiot?" Barry wagged his finger. "Every fraternity on this entire campus does a haunted house. We wouldn't stand a chance to win."

Adam wouldn't dream of joining one of the other fraternities. He only wanted to join Beta Alpha Nu Delta to meet fellow musicians.

"You pledges better come up with something brilliant by Halloween." Barry held his fist inches from Adam's nose. "That's two days away. If you fail and nobody shows up, don't expect an acceptance letter come Initiation. And you'll have me to reckon with."

Adam shuddered. College wasn't so different from high school after all.

###

Miguel Guzmán took a deep breath, then placed his fingers on the keys. The sound of the organ shattered the silence of the recital hall. He got the best practice room at the school, one of the advantages of being an organ major. Good thing, too. He needed the practice, considering the challenging set he'd planned for Mass on All Saints Day. Only a few days away. Normally it wasn't hard to choose repertoire for Sunday services. Play Bach and everyone would be happy. But this time he prayed the congregation wouldn't boo him from the balcony. What would they think of his prelude selection, Messiaen's "Apparition de l'église éternelle," or Jean Langlais' "Incantation pour un jour Saint" for postlude? Would they murder him for his modern taste? Not that he didn't enjoy the classics. But you could only play Bach so many times in a year and maintain your sanity.

The dissonant chords mirrored his mood. It had only been a year since the accident. He closed his eyes to block out the memory. Time to focus on the music at hand.

A knock wrenched him from his reverie. The door creaked open to reveal Adam Heckel standing in the doorway.

"A bit intense for Sunday church, don't you think?" Adam strode next to the organ bench.

Miguel sighed. "Oh no. If you as a music major think it's too much, what on earth will the priest say?"

Adam shrugged. "I wouldn't worry about it. Father Joseph seems pretty open-minded about music."

Miguel ran a hand through his thick black hair. "I hope you're right. When can I schedule you to play?"

Adam laughed. "You think they'd want to hear a bassoon solo?"

"Sure. You said Father Joseph likes new music."

"I suppose you could schedule me sometime in Advent. But in return, I need a favor."

"What kind?" Miguel frowned.

Adam shifted on the balls of his feet.

"Come on. I'm sure I'll say yes."

"All right. Here goes. I need you to play Bach's *Toccata and Fugue in D Minor* at a Halloween concert for Beta Alpha Nu Delta. I know you hate fraternities, and probably think the holiday is sacrilegious, but I'm out of options."

Miguel's breath caught in his throat. Didn't see that coming. "Why do you want to be in that frat anyway? I saw how they treated you and the other pledges last weekend. I want nothing to do with them."

Adam scrunched up his nose. "I was afraid you'd say that. Anything I can do to change your mind? Play two services during Advent?"

"It's not just the fraternity." Miguel dropped his gaze. "I have other plans that night."

"I see." Adam sighed. "Thought it was worth a shot. You know how everyone loves creepy organ music this time of year."

Miguel gritted his teeth. "Yes. I'm aware."

"Well, I'd better figure out something else before Barry decides to kill me." Adam turned to leave. "Sorry to interrupt your practice time."

###

Halloween night, Adam glanced around the nearly empty recital hall. So far, no one but his fellow pledge brothers had showed up for the Halloween concert. One of the trumpeters had dressed up as a ghost in what Adam guessed was a dirty sheet off his dorm room bed. A freshman clarinetist in a chicken suit was squawking through scales onstage. How appropriate.

Adam adjusted his own Grim Reaper costume. What was the point of spending fifty dollars on this outfit for no one to show up? Besides, he'd spent all day decorating the stage when he should've been practicing. A collection of jack-o-lanterns beamed from the sides, and a giant witch hung from the ceiling. In the center of the stage, he'd covered the old organ in faux cobwebs.

A second later, Barry barged through the recital hall doors dressed as Frankenstein's monster, followed by the rest of the upperclassmen in similar attire.

"Heckel, where's the audience?" He crossed his thick arms.

Adam glanced out the window where a large crowd of sorority girls clustered around the chili cook off table. Maybe he should've come up with a party that involved food rather than esoteric classical music. "I'm sorry."

"Sorry's not good enough." Barry yanked Adam's arms behind his back. "Hey, Russel, hand me the duct tape."

A guy in a wizard hat pulled a roll of duct tape from his cloak and handed it to Barry.

Adam flinched as the sticky material cemented his wrists together, followed by a strip over his mouth.

"Take him to my car." Barry barked. The wizard yanked him by the arms down the aisle and into the chilly night air.

"Get in." He shoved him into the back seat. Barry climbed into the driver's seat. "Looks like you won't get a bid after all."

###

Miguel punched the brakes of his old sedan as a group of trick-or-treaters crossed the street in front of him. Why'd they all wear such dark costumes instead of something easier to see at night? Obviously these kids hadn't grown up in a Hispanic home on *Día de los Muertos*.

He fingered his own suit covered in red and gold trim. Every year, he wore the traditional attire along with Mama's homemade *calavera* skull mask.

A few miles later, he pulled into a deserted cemetery and parked the car. Other than a few moonbeams which cast shadows through the trees, darkness enveloped the place. If anyone else saw him here, they'd think him crazy. But who cared? He wasn't doing this for them. Tonight he would honor Camila.

A lump formed in his throat as he grabbed the bouquet of marigolds from the passenger seat, along with a couple candles and a lighter. The holiday had been more fun in the past when he'd celebrated with his family. But this year was different. He brushed tears from his eyes as he marched toward his little sister's grave. The image of a semi crashing into their car flashed before his eyes. Only nine months since the accident.

A moment later, a loud moan pierced the silence. Who else would be here at this time of night? Was it some kind of Halloween prank? The cry rent the air again, louder than before.

Heartbeat pounding, Miguel squinted in the direction of the noise. For a moment he froze, rooted to the spot. "Who's there?"

"AAaaam," the muffled voice mumbled.

"Adam, is that you?" Miguel rushed to the tall obelisk where Adam sat duct-taped to the stone. Kneeling beside his friend, he pulled the tape from Adam's mouth. "What happened?"

"Barry and the other frat guys," Adam gasped. "They were furious about the turnout for the Halloween Concert, so they brought me here and left."

Miguel's heartbeat quickened as he scrambled to free Adam. "I knew they were scumbags, but I can't believe they'd sink this low. They should go to jail for this."

Tears streamed down Adam's cheeks. "I was stupid to want to be one of them."

Miguel pulled the last of the tape off Adam's wrists.

"Thanks." Adam shivered. "This place gives me the creeps."

"I suppose."

"It doesn't for you?" Adam's eyes grew large.

"Not really." Miguel shrugged. "I come here every year to visit my grandparents' graves. This place is my tie to history. It's part of the Hispanic way of life."

Adam gestured at the bouquet of flowers. "Is that why you brought those?"

Miguel shook his head. "Not tonight. These are for…"—he swallowed—"my sister. Camila."

"Oh, Miguel, I'm sorry. I didn't realize…"

"It's okay." He blinked back a tear. "She was only ten. I was supposed to protect her. I should've seen that truck coming." He winced. "I don't like to talk about it. It's still… You know."

"I get it." Adam patted him on the back. "I lost my older brother when I was a kid. He was my best friend. Always stood up for me at school. Once he was gone, nobody looked out for me anymore." He glanced at his wrist, still red from the tape.

Miguel nodded.

Adam rubbed his forehead. "Any chance you'd give me a ride back when you're done? No need to rush. I'll wait here."

Miguel placed a hand on his shoulder. “Come with me if you want. I could use a brother about now.”

“Really?” Adam’s eyes brightened.

“Yeah.”

As they walked in silence to Camila’s grave, the tightness in Miguel’s chest loosened. Maybe having a friend with him tonight was better than going through this alone. He needed a brother.

Miguel knelt beside the tombstone and pulled a picture of Camila and himself from his suit pocket.

“That’s her?” Adam knelt next to him. “Looks like you two were close.”

Miguel bit his lip, unable to form words. He laid the bouquet on the grave and handed the candles and lighter to Adam, who flicked on the flame and lit the wicks. For several moments, the two sat together in silence in the soft glow of the flickering candles.

“I suppose we’d better get back.” Miguel sighed. “I’ve got a concert to play.”

Adam jerked his head up. “What? There’s no way I’m going back.”

“I thought you wanted me to play Bach?”

“You told me no. Besides, don’t you play at Mass early tomorrow?”

Miguel chuckled. “Maybe I need a dress rehearsal. And I want to show those fake brothers of yours what a Halloween concert’s really like.”

###

Adam grinned at his reflection in Miguel's car mirror. "This is awesome! No one will recognize me. I can't believe you had a spare mask on hand."

Miguel laughed. "What'd you expect on *Día de los Muertos*?"

"The artistry on this skull is incredible." Adam leaned closer to the mirror. The lines swirled around his eyes and mouth in multiple directions.

"Mom made it for me years ago. She often gives them as gifts."

"Nice."

They pulled into the music school's parking lot. Outside, a crowd of people still clustered around the chili cook-off table. Even the BAND brothers.

Adam climbed out of the car. "Smells like they subbed alcohol for the chili."

Miguel clicked his door shut and hit the lock button. "Yeah, I'll bet they snuck in some booze."

A glance at a burly guy standing next to the table sent a shiver down Adam's spine. "Barry's chugging something. Don't let him see me."

Miguel nodded as he pulled out his phone. "Head inside the recital hall and make sure everything's ready for me."

Darkness enveloped Adam as he stepped into the empty room. Sure enough, all the others had bailed for the night for the more exciting party outside. Would anyone turn up if Miguel played? Or was it too late?

A couple minutes later, an eerie spotlight shone from the ceiling, illuminating the antique organ. Miguel crept out from a backstage door, an intimidating sight in his suit and mask. He climbed onto the bench, raised his hands above the cobwebbed keys, and began to play.

The strains of Bach's *Toccata and Fugue in D Minor* burst from the instrument like a phantom from a grave. Miguel must've pulled out all the stops.

The recital hall doors flew open. A dozen costumed students streamed inside, followed by the rest of the crowd, cups in hand. Guys dressed as zombies. Girls in slender black cat costumes. A few people looked familiar, but most Adam had never seen before. Must not have been from the music school. Why couldn't he have pulled this off sooner? What a turnout!

The intensity of the music rose as the batlike notes swirled around the hall. After Miguel reached the dramatic conclusion, the students jumped to their feet with applause. "Bravo, Beta Mu's," someone cheered.

Miguel took a deep bow.

Barry clambered onstage, a plastic cup clutched in his hands. "I wanna thank you all for coming today. My brothers and I have been planning this for weeks—"

Liar.

A police siren blared outside.

"Who called the cops?" A guy in a zombie outfit cried. "Let's get outta here."

The students poured out the door as quickly as they'd come. Several policemen barged into the room as Barry scrambled off the front of the stage.

Miguel pointed to him. "Here's your guy."

One of the cops rushed to Barry and pinned him to the ground. "He's the one who duct-taped the kid to the tombstone?"

With a swift motion, Miguel peeled off his mask. "Yep."

Barry gasped. "You connivin' little—"

"No time for that now." The policeman guided Barry to the exit. "You're coming with me. And we'll inform the college of your hazardous hazing. Don't plan to resume your frat for several weeks."

Barry scowled as the cop ushered him out the door.

Adam flashed Miguel a smile. "Thanks, man. I owe you."

Miguel clapped him on the back. "What's a friend for? But I'm sorry you won't have a fraternity to join anymore."

"It's ok. I know who my true brothers are." He grinned. "Thanks for bringing me Bach from the grave."

Get a “Händel” on It

A Christmas or Easter Story

Karen Schneider clambered through the sea of musicians to her assigned chair in the symphony hall. She gritted her teeth. Second chair. With a swift motion, she pulled her hundred-year-old violin from its case. The smell of antique wood filled the air. The varnish, faded after many years, contrasted with the shiny new instruments held by several other players. But for a violin, beauty increased with age.

The black dress Karen wore hid her non-existent hips like a grocery sack. She wiped damp palms on the chiffon fabric, then took her seat. *I hope the concert goes well today. For Angie's sake.* Karen scanned the assembled musicians in search of her sister. No sign of her yet.

Choir members in forest green robes filed onto risers, music binders in hand. Karen twirled a strand of hair around her finger, grateful to be in the orchestra pit and not on stage.

"Hello, Karen."

Her stomach muscles tightened at the curt voice beside her. Ugh, her stand partner, Sarah. "Good evening."

The girl ran a manicured hand through raven black hair. "Ready for tonight?"

Karen rubbed her forehead. "Yes. Are you?"

"Of course." Sarah straightened her shoulders. I've performed Handel's *Messiah* a dozen times. I could play it in my sleep."

Ever since Sarah transferred to Belton University from Chicago, she'd sat first chair for every concert. *How unfair.* Karen had spent her entire life in this college town. But now "*Miss Big City*" had swept in and taken over.

The conductor commanded his place on the platform and motioned for Sarah to tune. She flashed a radiant smile, then played the tuning note as long as possible.

Diva.

Karen held her breath as she waited for the maestro's opening cue. At the stroke of his downbeat, she pulled her bow across the strings. The strains of the minor theme filled the spacious concert hall with life and sound. All thoughts of Sarah faded as Karen focused her energy on the music at hand. The notes, fast and powerful, burst from her instrument like horses from a starting gate.

After the lively first movement, the tenor soloist, dressed in a crisp black tux, crooned the words "Comfort Ye My People." Karen drew a deep breath. After such a volatile winter, especially with the death of her aunt, she relished the comfort of the ancient words. Music served as the balm to her heartache. She'd been Karen's first violin teacher—the one who'd encouraged her to become a music major. How she missed her aunt's guidance, coffee dates, and late-night chats. Tears threatened to spill. Now who would champion her career, with her aunt gone and Sarah's domination of the music scene?

A couple measures of rests afforded Karen the chance to glance at the vocalists. Why hadn't Angie joined the other soloists on stage? She'd never miss a concert. Karen scanned the back of the stage again to find her sister. The drummer, George, gave her a wink. His shaggy hair hung like curtains around his face. Heat crept into her cheeks as hypothetical visions of the two of them alone backstage filled her mind. As both a classical percussionist and drummer in a rock band, he'd won the title "heartthrob" of the music school. If only he'd ask her out.

A jab in the arm from Sarah's bow jerked her back to the present. Time for the violins to take the melody. As the they began the theme "For Unto Us a Child Is Born," a horrible squawk erupted from Sarah's instrument. She pulled it from her shoulder, her face drained of all color. The E string had snapped.

They both froze. How could Sarah lead the section without one of her strings?

For one brilliant second, Karen's heart leapt. *This is my chance. I can lead the orchestra without her.*

That same moment, her sister Angie strode onstage, a radiant soprano in a satin dress that accentuated her curves. Of course she'd waited until her solo to make a grand appearance.

Angie flashed her a smile, but it quickly faltered at the sight of the broken string.

"Do something," she mouthed to Karen.

She sighed. Although nothing would give her more pleasure than to watch Sarah sit in silence while Karen led the violin section, it wasn't protocol. Her gaze dropped to the antique instrument in her hands. Could she trust anyone else with this treasure? She closed her eyes, exhaled, then extended her precious instrument to Sarah.

The look of panic on her face softened to one of gratitude. For a split second, their eyes met. "Thank you," Sarah mouthed as they exchanged instruments.

"You're welcome."

Sarah clutched the violin under her chin and motioned for the rest of the section to join.

Karen opened her own rectangular case and dug in one of the compartments. *I've got a spare set of strings in here somewhere.* She pulled out a thin spiral wire and threaded it through the hole in the peg. After several turns, the wood twisted into position, just as Angie opened with "Rejoice, Rejoice, Rejoice Greatly." Karen's lips curved into a smile as she rejoiced that she could still accompany her sister, whose beautiful voice reverberated throughout the hall like Easter bells.

During Intermission, Sarah and Karen swapped instruments backstage.

"Thanks for saving me back there." Sarah bit her lip. "I'm glad you had a spare string on hand. I forgot to replace mine."

Karen shrugged. "No problem. Glad to help."

Sarah smiled. "You'd make a good section leader. Maybe we can trade places sometime if the conductor agrees to it. Your violin is already used to first chair."

Karen laughed. "I wouldn't say no."

"You wouldn't?" A deep voice sounded behind her.

She spun around to find herself face-to-face with George.

"In that case, how about dinner with me after the concert?" He ran his hand through his shaggy hair. Her heart beat as fast as a drumroll.

"Uhhh…" Her voice caught in her throat.

He placed a hand on her shoulder. "I'll take that as a yes." With a quick stride, he returned to his place behind the timpani.

"Let's go." Sarah pulled her back onstage. "We don't want to be late."

As Karen settled into second chair, excitement welled up in her chest at the prospect of leading the orchestra, not to mention a date with George. At this rate she might as well join the choir for the "Hallelujah Chorus."

Christmas Glee Club

A Christmas Story

Sophia sighed as she slipped into her red velvet Santa baby dress, accented with white fur trim. Bustling sounds of her sorority sisters' preparations for their Christmas party filled the spacious room. One in a green boho dress zipped up another's much-too-slinky black cocktail dress. Why did the Belton Glee Club have to perform today, the night of the party?

A glance at the mirror on the opposite wall revealed a smudge of mascara under Sophia's eye. She knocked shoes aside on her way to the vintage vanity against the wall. Several makeup bags already cluttered the surface. Good thing she'd received a bright purple one for her last birthday, which made it easy to spot. She unzipped the bag, pulled out a cotton ball and makeup remover to dab the smudge, and then retrieved her mascara to reapply.

A second later, someone hip-bumped her out of the way, and she smeared mascara all over her eye.

"Hey, watch it!" Sophia turned and found herself face-to-face with Lauren Preston, who wore the slinky black dress.

Lauren's eyes traveled up and down Sophia's outfit. She quirked an eyebrow. "Looks like Mrs. Claus is coming to our party tonight. Are you bringing candy canes for everyone?"

The muscles in Sophia's stomach tightened. "No. This is my outfit for Glee Club. I'll be late to the party because we have a gig. But I've got another dress to wear after the show."

Lauren's eyes narrowed. "What does your date think of this? Who are you bringing, anyway?"

"Jaydn Daniels."

"You're kidding." A frown creased Lauren's brow. "The star basketball player? I asked him, but he said he was going with someone else."

Inwardly, Sophia's heart did a little happy dance. She'd beaten snooty Lauren Preston, sorority social chair, to the hottest date on campus. But because of this stupid gig, now she'd be more than fashionably late. What would a star athlete think of missing half the party while waiting for her?

"Sorry, Lauren, I've got to finish up here. I have to be at the Alumni Donor Christmas Gala in twenty minutes to warm up."

"Have fun." Lauren sneered while she sauntered away in her high heels.

###

Brett blew on his fingers as he clambered from his car to James Belton Hall. Bright Christmas lights illuminated the historic administrative building while its golden dome gleamed in the moonlight. Since his first year at Belton, he'd loved the ambiance of the historic school—like time-travel to a previous era.

He quickened his pace to prevent his throat from constricting due to the cold. He'd need every ounce of breath support to hit the high tenor notes. Not that he played an important role by any means. Mike always landed the solos. And duets. Why'd he get to play Santa with Sophia on his lap while the rest of them dressed as elves? Lucky dog. Brett's cheeks warmed at the thought of Sophia in her velvet red Santa Baby dress. Man was she out of his league!

After a hard tug on the massive front door, he slid inside and padded down the hallway to the banquet room.

Inside the spacious venue, donors milled around in formal attire. Men in crisp suits and tuxedos escorted ladies in shimmering evening gowns. An enormous Christmas tree with elaborate ornaments and bright white lights stood to the side of the stage. Members of the BAND music fraternity served hors d'oeuvres and fancy pastries from shiny silver platters, while others passed out sparkling beverages. Good community service after their Halloween fiasco.

A tap on his shoulder, Brett spun around. Professor Winston, the choir director, stood in front of him. Beads of sweat dripped down the man's cheeks, which he mopped with a handkerchief. "Brett. You're up tonight. Mike's got laryngitis. Can't sing a note."

Brett gasped. "What? You want me?" After two-and-a-half years as Brett's choir director, he'd never once offered Brett the solo. That had always been Mike's job.

"You're the only one who knows his part. I can't pass it to one of the basses, can I?" Professor Winston shoved a black bag into Brett's hands.

"What's this?" Brett ran his hands over the lumpy sack.

Professor Winston rolled his eyes. "Your Santa costume, of course. It might be baggy, but should work. Now get changed. We're on in fifteen."

###

"And now, ladies and gentlemen, let's give a round of applause for the Belton Glee Club." The president clapped his hands together while several donors tinkled their glasses. Sophia sighed. About time. His speech had lasted much longer than she'd anticipated. At this rate she'd never make it to the Christmas party.

While Sophia waited backstage for her solo, other members of the choir strolled onstage singing "It's Beginning to Look a lot like Christmas" in elf costumes. She ran her hands over the folds of her dress. At least she didn't have to wear pointy green shoes and striped candy cane pants like the others. What was Jaydn thinking right now? She'd spent hardly any time with him, but the fact he'd said yes to her was a good sign. Although what guy would turn down a free sorority T-shirt?

Minutes later, the elves launched into "Here We Come A-Caroling" in rich, four-part harmony. Almost time for Santa's big entrance. Hopefully Mike wasn't drunk or hungover like last time. What a nightmare.

The group started "Santa Claus is Comin' to Town," the rich harmonies filling the air. Santa bumped into her as he brushed past.

She scowled. "Watch it, Mike."

Blue eyes twinkled below the white trim of the Santa hat. "I'm not Mike. I'm St. Nick." The guy winked and hurried onstage.

If it wasn't Mike, where on earth was he? And who'd Professor Winston chosen to take his place? It had to be Brett. But did he even know how to sing solos? And how could she sing the winter medley duets with Brett when they'd never practiced together?"

A ping from her phone caught her attention. A message from Lauren.

Hey, my date's sick, so I'm taking Jaydn to the formal. I figured you wouldn't mind, since you can't make it anyway. See you later.

Ugh. Could this evening get any worse?

###

"Ho, Ho, Ho," Brett bellowed, striding to the front of the stage. "Looks like we've got a glittering assembly of merrymakers here tonight." He gestured at an elderly lady who'd nearly blinded him with her sequined gown.

"I hope you've all been good because you're in for a special treat with this next number. Let's give it up to welcome Santa Sophia to the stage."

His breath caught in his throat at the sight of her. The velvet red dress with white trim really accentuated her curves.

"Thanks, Santa." Sophia's chocolate eyes beamed at him. "Why don't you take a seat on this chair, and I'll let you know what I want for Christmas." She tugged him into the black folding chair and plopped onto his lap. Wow, it was warm in here, especially in this costume.

She launched into a hilarious rendition of "Santa Baby," asking for everything from makeup and an iPhone to a brand-new car. How he wanted to stroke her long blonde hair while the coquettish soprano filled his ears. Better stick to a smile and a nod.

###

Sophia breathed a sigh of relief. So far, so good. At least Brett proved an adequate actor. But now for the true test. How well could he perform their winter duets?

"Mrs. Claus"—he rose from the chair—"would you do me the honor of joining me for this next number?" With a smooth motion he extended his hand to her. "I believe it's snowing outside."

With a toss of her hair, she took his proffered hand. "Let it snow, as long as I'm with you, Santa." She'd recited those words a hundred times before, but this time the line brought a tingling sensation. How could Brett exert such an effect on her?

Heart drumming, they strolled hand in hand for "Marshmallow World." His fingers intertwined in hers like garland laced with Christmas lights, igniting her on the inside.

For their second song, "Let It Snow," the choreography called for him to stand behind and wrap his arms around her waist. Now she'd never be able to concentrate! His muscular arms enveloped her, and she leaned back against his firm chest. No Santa gut on this guy.

By their final number, "Baby, It's Cold Outside," her heartbeat quickened to the pace of jingle bells on steroids. Surely this was nothing. A crush. He placed his hand on the small of her back, and they began to dance. Although the lyrics of the song protested his proximity with every word, her heart melted as his gaze met hers. Tonight, she was supposed to be on a date with the star basketball player, not falling for Brett, the backup tenor. But with his vocals and magical touch, he could outperform Santa Mike any day.

As the song progressed, Brett's grip on her tightened. He drew her to him, so close the scent of woodsy cologne filled her nostrils. Intoxicating. Could she resist his charms, or would she fall for him, like the woman in "Baby It's Cold Outside?"

###

Brett racked his brain for the final lyrics to the song. How could he focus with Sophia wrapped up in his arms? For a moment, he froze. What were his words? Sophia's gaze bored into his. What should he do?

No use, the lyrics had completely escaped him. A look of panic crossed Sophia's beautiful features. Only one thing left to do.

Like a swing dancer from the jazz era, he twirled her into him, dipped her low, and kissed her. Never mind all the alumni donors watching, let alone the president of Belton, and the entire Glee Club. Right now, those gorgeous red lips kissing him back blocked everything else from his mind.

When they broke apart, a cheer and wolf-whistles erupted from the other choir members who joined the couple onstage. Not a bad save after all.

###

Sophia's breath caught in her throat. Of course she'd been kissed before, but never like that. No one could fake that level of intensity. Her mind whirred as she sang the final song, "We Wish You a Merry Christmas," with the rest of the choir. After their last bow, she followed the flurry of singers offstage.

Brett pulled her behind the curtain, a look of concern on his face. "I hope I wasn't too bad tonight. Sorry I had to fill in at the last second."

She ran a hand through her hair. “No, you weren’t bad at all. Your tenor harmonies were superb.”

“Thanks.” He traced a finger along her arm. “But I didn’t mean the vocals.” His eyes twinkled at her.

“Ah.” Her heart fluttered. “You’re fishing for another compliment, aren’t you?”

He brushed a stray hair from her face. “I figured you wouldn’t kiss like that just for a show.”

By now, her cheeks burned with the warmth of his touch.

“Maybe I’m a good actress.” She batted her eyelashes.

“Not that good.” He pulled her in for another kiss.

Sophia melted into him as his lips explored hers, his arms wrapped around her. After several more glorious moments, the two broke apart.

He grinned. “I’ve been dying to do that for months. Can’t believe you kissed me back.”

She brushed another kiss on his cheek.

The Santa hat cocked sideways over his forehead, allowing a strand of his shaggy dark hair to protrude. “What do you want to do now?”

“Hmm.” She pursed her lips together. “I was supposed to attend my sorority formal tonight, but I’ve already missed half of it, and my roommate stole my date, Jaydn Bolton.”

His eyebrows raised. “The basketball player?”

She nodded. “By the time I change and fix my stage makeup, it’ll be over.”

Brett fingered the heavy backstage curtain. “I have an idea. What if you don’t change, and I escort you to the party myself?”

“Dressed like Santa?”

“Sure. I’ll bet Santa’s got more clout than a basketball star.” His smile widened.

“But I look ridiculous in this dress.” She scrunched her nose. “Like Mrs. Claus.”

He offered his elbow to escort her. “Perfect. Let’s go, Mrs. Claus.”

The Ivory Touch

A Winter or Spring Story

Pauline brushed a mass of curls away from her face as she watched the February snow swirl outside the window of the cramped practice room. The baby grand piano filled every inch of the limited space.

When she took a deep breath, she choked from the musty wood smell. If only the staff at Belton University would clean these rooms once in a while. She sighed. Nothing to do about that now.

Her senior recital, the capstone of her collegiate career, loomed only a month away. As a result, Pauline practically lived in this room. Might as well set up a cot and move in. What if she failed to perform the hour-long program well enough to graduate? And now her teacher insisted that Pauline add another piece. How could she possibly prepare it in time?

Her hands flitted over the ivory keys as she played the opening of Rachmaninov's *Piano Sonata No. 1*. The first, halting notes filled the room with an eerie sense of foreboding. Pauline shuddered. What possessed her to choose such a difficult work in the first place? A battle of nerves raged inside when she pounded through the fast passages. As her fingers flew over the keys, she succumbed to the magic of the music. The tension in her neck lessoned as the beautiful strains filled the room. The music pushed away all thoughts of the deadly virus which had already spread its vicious tentacles through China had infected Europe as well. The muscles in her stomach tightened. *Nana.* Her grandmother had travelled to Italy a few days ago to perform a concert. Hopefully the illness wouldn't affect her travel.

Time to focus. Pauline's hands swirled over the keys like the Midwestern blizzard raging outside. Her tendons ached from so many hours of practice, but she couldn't give up now, not with graduation on the line.

The door banged open, and a trumpet blast shredded the air.

"Trenton, you scared me." She gasped. "I was in the middle of the Rachmaninov."

A mischievous grin spread across Trenton's dark, handsome face. Her boyfriend set his trumpet on the lone chair and moved to the piano. A shiver tingled down her spine as his strong, muscular arms slid around her waist. For a moment, all thoughts of the recital melted away as she leaned back against his firm chest.

He ran a hand through her curls and massaged her head. "You sound awesome. Why don't you take a break?"

She spun around on the bench to face him. "Are you serious? My professor insisted I add another song to the program—the Chopin Waltz wasn't 'modern' enough for my finale."

He shrugged. "Throw in a jazz number like I did for mine."

She rolled her eyes. "I don't think *Professor Piano Queen* will consider jazz an acceptable alternative."

"All right. Play a duet with me."

Pauline pursed her lips. "Be serious. We'd never get anything done." He drew her closer, but she pushed him away.

He raised an eyebrow. "I *am* serious. I'd love to play with you." He pulled her to him again.

How could she resist those pleading chestnut eyes and his rich, black skin? "Do you have a song in mind?"

"Yep." He sprang to the door and yanked it open. "Be right back."

Surely he wouldn't suggest one of their pieces from the jazz ensemble. Heat crept into her cheeks at the thought of their first rehearsal together last year. She'd joined the group at the last minute because their pianist underwent carpal tunnel surgery three days before the Valentine's Day concert.

That night, Pauline lost her place when Trenton crooned the solo "My Funny Valentine" on his trumpet. The pure, clear tone of his instrument combined with his innovative improv skills mesmerized her.

"You play like a suburban princess," he told her after the rehearsal. "Give it more swing."

"I'm a classical pianist," she laughed. "Not a flapper girl."

"No worries." He winked. "I'll teach you. It's time you prepare for the upcoming era, the roaring 2020s."

Pauline giggled at the memory. Now, a year later, she and Trenton were still dating, taking on the new decade together.

He burst through the door again, a score in hand. "Here." He plopped the music onto the piano.

Pauline's breath caught in her throat. The title, *Sonata for Piano and Trumpet* by Hindemith, glared at her from the page. She shook her head. "No. We'll never prepare it in time. I didn't even know he wrote a piece for piano and trumpet. It'll be too dissonant."

"Come on, Pauline." He rubbed her back. "Your teacher wants modern music. A twentieth-century German composer fits the bill, unless she meant contemporary."

Pauline sighed. "All right, let's give it a try." She traced his stubbled chin with her forefinger. "But be warned, my graduation rides on this last piece."

He caught her hand in his and held her gaze. "I know. But we can do it together. I promise."

Dear God, I hope he's right.

###

Pauline hung her coat on the peg next to the front door of her apartment. The scent of pizza and brownies wafted through the air. How delicious. Her roommates must've made dinner. She glanced at her watch. Eleven o'clock. No wonder she was hungry. She hurried to the kitchen and rummaged for the half-eaten pan of brownies, cut off a square, and headed to her room.

Her bed, covered in a light purple comforter and several throw pillows, called to her. She flopped down and hugged a pillow to her chest. The cozy room exuded comfort—a place to escape the pressures of the practice room. Pictures of her family and friends adorned her desk.

The rehearsal with Trenton, although rough, went better than she'd expected. The difficult piece would require extra practice, but Trenton seemed eager for the challenge. Either that or he wanted time with her. These past few weeks she'd been so busy with rehearsal, they hadn't had much romance.

He'd been busy, too, preparing for *his* senior recital. But he'd always found time for dates—early mornings before class, late nights at the coffee shop after practice. What would happen to their relationship after graduation? An engagement? Or would they go their separate ways? She winced at the thought. She'd grown used to his encouragement, his perpetual smile, his touch. Her heartbeat quickened. If he planned to propose, he was running out of time. Graduate music schools expected her response by April.

Her phone chimed an alert as "Nana" flashed on the screen. Why would she call so late? Oh, right, it was already morning in Italy. Thank goodness for free long-distance calls.

"*Buongiorno*, Nana."

"*Buongiorno*, my dear," Nana's voice trilled. "Did I call too late?"

"Of course not." Pauline snuggled under the covers, still wearing her clothes.

The connection crackled. "How are you?" Nana asked.

"Busy. I spend all my time at the music school." Pauline twisted her hands in her lap.

"Ah yes. You're preparing for your recital. What is your repertoire?"

Pauline tightened her grip on the pillow. "Mozart, Rachmaninov, and Hindemith."

"How ambitious," Nana said in a cheerful manner. "I'm sure you'll be fabulous."

"I hope so." Pauline stroked the soft folds of the comforter. "You'll be back by then, won't you?"

Silence.

"Nana, are you there?" A twinge of worry clawed at the back of Pauline's mind.

"Yes, dear. I'm here. But this is why I called. Italy has closed its borders."

Pauline froze. "Nana, you can't be serious. Why?"

"The virus has spread throughout the country. Many people have already died, and more do so every day."

Pauline blinked several times. How was this possible? "But Nana, I'm sure they'll let you go, won't they? When is your concert?"

"Canceled. All concerts, public events, and large gatherings are prohibited."

Fear gripped Pauline like an iron fist. How could the government cancel all public events in an entire country? What if Nana couldn't leave?

"Nana, come back. Do whatever you need in order to return home. I can't play this recital without you."

Nana groaned. "I'll try, dear, but I can't make any promises. They may allow some flights for repatriation. We can pray."

Pauline stifled a sob. "I will."

###

Two weeks later, Pauline trudged down the narrow hallway to the practice rooms, the past several days a blur. She couldn't wrap her mind around all that had happened. Although she and Trenton practiced together two hours each day, the Hindemith Sonata didn't reach her high level of expectation.

She cringed as she turned the doorknob to the practice room. How many people had touched this handle today? What kind of germs lived on it? In the past, she'd never worried about such matters. But news that the Coronavirus had spread to the American Midwest plunged the entire university into a panic. Students carried antibacterial hand gel in their instrument cases. Teachers set up soap dispensers in classrooms.

A rumor spread that they'd gain an extra week of spring break to let the virus pass. An additional week of practice before her recital might be useful. But when would the panic stop? And what about Nana?

A few days ago, the airlines granted her grandmother a flight back to the United States. However, the seventy-year-old was placed under quarantine upon arrival. What if she couldn't attend Pauline's recital in a few weeks? Worse, what if she'd contracted the virus? A queasy feeling of uneasiness stole over Pauline.

Inside, the smell of body odor mixed with antique wood and dust nearly overpowered her and caused her to gag.

"Are you all right?" Trenton's deep voice echoed behind her.

She spun to face him and flung her arms around his neck. "I'm scared. It seems the whole world has fallen to pieces." She breathed in the scent of his rich cologne, woodsy mixed with spice. "The university might close for a couple of weeks, the stores are out of toilet paper, and Nana's in quarantine. I don't know what to think."

As Trenton rubbed her shoulders, the tension in her arms eased. "It'll be okay. We have each other, and that's what counts. Besides, you can always use leaves."

She drew back. "What?"

"Leaves. For toilet paper." His impish grin returned.

"You're crazy."

"We all are these days." He squatted next to his trumpet case and retrieved his instrument. After wetting his lips, he held the metal to his mouth.

Pauline moved to the piano. "Ready?"

He nodded.

This time, they performed the piece in perfect synchronization. She anticipated his every move, and he kept time with her. As she pounded the powerful chords, the dissonance she once considered jarring now gave vent to her feelings about the uncertainty of the times. In an odd, indescribable way, the music was the conduit to her voice lost in the chaos of a crumbling world.

She poured her soul into the keys, playing each note with added emotion. When they approached the climax, her heartbeat quickened. Beads of sweat trickled down Trenton's temples. Their eyes met. For a second, she forgot about the moment and relished the comfort of his gaze. He nodded, and they finished the final chord together with a flourish.

Several seconds of pause ensued. Heat spread to her cheeks from the exhilaration of the performance. Finally, Trenton set his trumpet on the piano, his breathing heavy. "We … made … it," he panted.

She dropped her gaze, willing her adrenaline to subside. "Yes. Perfect performance."

"Pauline"—he hesitated, then slid next to her on the bench—"I wondered…"

"Yes?" She lifted her eyes to his.

"I—"

The door banged open. A wind ensemble player stood there, clarinet in hand. "They've closed the school."

Trenton jumped up. "For an extra week?"

The clarinetist's eyes clouded as he shook his head. "No. For the rest of the school year."

###

Pauline slumped on the plush couch in her parents' living room. Pictures Dad took on his worldwide travels as a professional photographer adorned the walls—Tower Bridge in London, the Great Wall of China, the Eiffel Tower in Paris.

A sigh escaped her lips. In the short week she'd been home, every country had sealed its borders. Who knew if she'd ever visit those exotic places Dad loved so much.

Belton University had issued an emergency order to send everyone home right away. They didn't want students to contract the virus from living and studying in close quarters.

She'd barely found time to pack, let alone say goodbye to her friends. And Trenton… Her heart cried in protest. He'd returned to his parents' home on the East Coast. Tears wet the corners of her eyes. Who knew when they'd see each other again?

At least they talked every day. Yesterday they'd gone on a virtual date to a zoo that hosted live field trips. She'd enjoyed it but missed his calm presence and reassuring embrace.

And what about her recital? How ridiculous to worry about something so trivial in light of the global crisis. But she'd worked hard to master every nuance of those beautiful works, and for what? To have the notes die along with her dreams of the future? She buried her face in her hands as sobs overtook her.

Minutes later, she wiped her eyes and moved to Mom's baby grand by the bay window. She hadn't practiced in days, but maybe now was the time. Pauline took a deep breath and played the ivories. The first strains of Chopin's *Waltz in c# minor* filled the living room, the minor key reflecting her dismal mood. Rich tones struck a chord deep within her that unleashed her pent-up fear. The music reflected her grief about the loss of her senior year, the end of an era. She closed her eyes as her fingers danced over the keyboard, free to roam wherever they pleased—unlike her.

A hand brushed her arm. She turned to see Mom, tears streaming down her gentle face.

An icy chill stole through Pauline. "What's wrong? Is it Nana?"

Mom nodded as she struggled to stifle sobs. "Nana has a confirmed case of the virus. She's in the local hospital for breathing treatment." Mom collapsed on the bench. "The virus is worse for senior citizens. I hope she can survive." She burst into sobs.

Pauline enveloped Mom in her arms. *Dear God, please let Nana live.*

###

A week later, now mid-March, the satin material of Pauline's white concert dress swished at her sides as she stepped up to the baby grand in her parents' living room. How different she'd imagined this day—the recital hall at the music school filled with her professors, family, and friends— Trenton. And Nana. A tear threatened to fall. *Keep it together. Power through. For Nana.*

Dad, who'd promised to send the recording to her professor as credit for graduation, situated his video camera on a tripod. How anticlimactic.

Mom smiled as she propped a computer on the coffee table. The previous day, she'd insisted Pauline conduct a live, virtual recital online.

"No one wants to watch an hour-long classical piano performance on a phone," Pauline protested.

"People crave hope in periods of uncertainty," Mom said. "During this time of limited physical contact, your sweet ivory touch might offer comfort to those in isolation."

Perhaps Mom was right. Maybe this was her contribution to a world in pain.

She adjusted her skirt and drew in a deep breath. *Dear God, let this music soothe the pain and suffering we face in the world today. Amen.*

Dad gave her a thumbs up behind the camera. Time to start.

The gentle, familiar notes of Mozart's Sonata No. 11 rang through the room, calming her nerves. The tension in her hands loosened as the nostalgic theme filled her with thoughts of a more peaceful time.

The many hours of practice on the Rachmaninov paid off as her fingers flew over the keys. After its conclusion, she paused for a moment. The next song should have been her duet with Trenton. If only he were here with her. Instead of the Hindemith, she'd substituted the Chopin Waltz. She raised her hands—

The sound of *Trumpet Voluntary* blasted from the entryway. Pauline glanced at the door where Trenton stood poised in a black tux, trumpet pressed to his lips. She jumped to her feet and ran to him.

"Hold on, I haven't finished my solo yet." He laughed.

"I've heard it before." She giggled as she threw her arms around his neck. "How'd you get here? I thought people were required to stay home with their families."

A wide grin spread across his face. "That's why I'm here." He dropped to one knee. "To ask you to be my family, during this quarantine, and for the rest of our lives." He pulled a tiny box from his pocket. "Pauline, will you marry me?"

Electricity sparked through her arm as he slipped the diamond ring on her finger.

A fountain of emotion bubbled up from somewhere deep inside. She wouldn't have to face this scary world alone. "Yes, yes!"

He pulled her in for a kiss, and she tightened the embrace, savoring the moment and the taste of his lips.

When they broke apart several glorious moments later, a loud cheer erupted from the computer. Mom flipped it around to reveal the audience as they applauded the couple.

Pauline gasped as she knelt in front of the computer. "Mom, you knew." The sight of her college roommates, piano professor, friends from the university, and Nana took her breath away.

Nana waved. Pauline's heart leapt. "Nana, how did you manage to watch this?"

A nurse in a crisp white uniform replied. "Easy. Your grandma insisted you were playing a recital she couldn't miss, so we connected the TVs to your link. The whole hospital watched you perform. Bravo! You've been an inspiration to us all."

Tears streamed freely down Pauline's cheeks. "Thanks. It's the least I could do."

The nurse arched an eyebrow. "Now Nana wants to meet this fiancé of yours—make sure he's good enough for her girl."

Trenton popped onto the screen. "I assure you, I'm not." He laughed. "But I'll do my best to take care of your granddaughter."

Nana's eyes sparkled as she nodded.

"Should we finish with our duet?" Trenton gave Pauline's hand a squeeze.

She met his gaze as she strode to the piano. "Do you think we can do this?"

He raised his trumpet. "Absolutely. We're in this together."

No Strings Attached

A Valentine's Story

The rank smell of body odor and musty wood filled Vince's nostrils as he lowered the viola to his side. A glance at his watch showed 7:45 p.m. He'd been practicing for two hours already, and for what? A botched version of this orchestral excerpt. *Yep, pretty sure it sounded worse than before.* The bare white walls of the practice room seemed to close in around him. Time for a couple minutes of break from this musical jail cell.

After he laid the instrument in its case, Vince yanked open the door. Why was the building so empty? Students practiced until at least ten most nights. As he meandered down the hallway to the vending machine, a few trombone blasts accosted his ears. So, Vince wasn't the only one practicing tonight after all.

He inserted a couple of bills and selected a candy bar and a bag of chips.

"Not much of a dinner on Valentine's Day, is it?"

Vince spun around and found himself face-to-face with Tristan, trombone in hand.

"Hello," Vince muttered.

Tristan grunted. "You planning on splitting the candy bar with someone? Pretty cheap date, I'd say."

Vince shrugged. "I don't see you here with anyone."

"I have reservations for 8:30." Tristan fingered the valves of the trombone as if trying to eek out a few more moments of practice. "At Lucianos on Main Street. They were booked solid until then."

Vince nodded.

"I'd better get going." Tristan clapped his hand on Vince's shoulder. "Wouldn't want to keep my date waiting. I'll let you get back to your date with *Viola.*" He snickered.

Anger bubbled up inside Vince. "Based on the shrieking noises blasting from your practice room, I'd say you need a date with your instrument, too."

Tristan scowled before he stomped off.

Vince creaked open the door to his practice room, his insides churning. It was Valentine's Day, the reason for the nearly empty building. How did everyone manage to find a date except him? Even Tristan. A glance at the excerpt on the music stand almost made him gag on his candy bar. He couldn't look at that passage anymore tonight. But where could he go? All the restaurants would be booked with lovey-dovey couples. No use even trying one of those. Maybe the coffee shop would still have a few seats available. At least there he could bury his head in a book and avoid attracting attention to his lonely state. Yes, that would be best.

###

Bells jingled as Gaby pulled open the door to Café Chocolat. She propped it open with her foot and maneuvered her guitar case through the entrance as the sweet smell of coffee and chocolate greeted her senses. Her stomach rumbled. Maybe she should've eaten dinner before coming. But she was scheduled to play in fifteen minutes. No time for food now. Besides, the line for coffee and pastries nearly reached the door. Apparently every couple at Belton University had chosen this place to spend Valentine's Day. Ugh. Worst holiday of the year. Why did society have to highlight all the happy couples in the world? This day made singles stand out like a harpist in a rock band.

Gaby pushed several heart decorations dangling from the ceiling out of her face as she made her way to the wall behind the stage. The guy at the mic, in a light pink button-down shirt and khaki pants, crooned love songs.

Her own tattered jeans and black T-shirt didn't exactly scream Valentine's Day. She squatted, set her guitar case on the floor, and clicked open the latches. Hopefully the strings hadn't slipped too much with the February cold.

A few minutes later, prep boy finished, and the crowd erupted with applause. A wide grin spread across his face as he took a bow.

"Encore," a girl at the front table shouted.

"I'd love to, but I've gotta make room for the next act." He gestured for Gaby to take the stage.

She lowered herself onto the stool in front of the mic, then propped her guitar on her thigh. The strings rang out as she tuned all six to their proper pitches. Bells jingled as the entrance door opened, and a tall guy stepped inside with a bulky case. Definitely not a guitar but too big to be a mandolin or ukulele. What was it?

###

Vince's ears perked up as the strains of acoustic guitar filled the room. A girl with shaggy, brunette hair sat perched on a wooden stool, hunched over the instrument. Her dark attire stood in stark contrast to the bright reds and pinks worn by most of the other coffeehouse patrons. A tattoo of music notes on a staff swiveled all the way up her right arm.

After several moments of meticulous tuning, the girl leaned into the mic.

"Hi, I'm Gaby, and I'm going to play a few originals tonight. This first one is called 'Lizards in the Land.'"

Hmm. Should be interesting. Not at all what he'd expected for a Valentine's Day concert. He liked this girl more and more every minute.

Her tattooed arm dropped to strum several loud chords, then her edgy voice knocked him back a few steps. Several girls in front covered their ears. A couple at a high top in the back stood to leave. Fortuitous, since Vince hadn't spotted any other open seats. He set his viola case on the floor at his feet and sat at the now-vacated table. Elbows propped and chin in his hands, he listened, mesmerized. Her sound was unlike anything he'd ever heard at the music school. True, her voice lacked classical training and finesse, but her breath-support was incredible, and her intonation spot-on.

###

After the conclusion of "Lizards of the Land" several couples stood up to leave. Gaby's heart sank when the same thing happened after the next couple of songs. What if the whole cafe cleared out during her set? They'd never let her play here again. She should've known that a Frenchy place like Café Chocolat wasn't the venue for her alternative style.

"I've got one more number for you guys, then I'll leave you to your dates and coffee. This next song is "'Artists' Escape'."

"Wish I could make my escape," a guy said from a table to the left. His date held a mug to her lips and giggled.

Tears threatened to spill down Gaby's cheeks. Why'd she let these guys get to her? She'd never allowed other people's opinions to affect her before. Her pride rested in her independence and originality— not in popular appeal. Still, it'd be nice if *someone* liked her music.

She finished up the last few chords, then stood up. "That's it for me tonight."

"Thank goodness," a girl in a fuchsia sweater muttered.

Head down, Gaby returned to her guitar case. What a disastrous night.

"Nice job."

"What?" She looked up to see the guy with the weird instrument standing over her.

He leaned his free arm against the wall. "I said nice job."

She turned back to her case and latched it shut. "No need to lie. I know everyone hated it."

"I didn't."

"Look." She grabbed her instrument case and stood. "I'm not in the mood for flirting, flattery, or whatever."

His brow furrowed. "I… uh …wasn't trying to do either. I don't believe in flattery, and I've never been a good flirt."

A smile tugged at the corner of her mouth. *Was this guy a joke*?

"Look, I legitimately liked your songs. I've played music my whole life, and I've never heard a sound like yours. So authentic and hard core."

The knot in Gaby's stomach loosened. "Okay. I'll pretend to believe you. What instrument is that anyway?" She pointed to the case strapped to his back.

"Oh this?" He slung it forward. "Guess."

"Hmm." Her eyebrows knitted as she squinted to examine it. "Violin?"

"Close. Viola."

"What's the difference?"

"They're similar, but the viola is bigger and plays lower notes than the violin."

"I've never seen one before."

"I'm not surprised." He laughed. "A lot of people haven't. Want to hear it? We could have a jam session."

She frowned. Was he hitting on her?

"Not a date, if that's why you're worried." He stepped back a few paces. "No strings attached. I promise."

A laugh escaped her lips. Not a bad line from a fellow string player. "Sure, why not? I'm Gaby, by the way."

"Vince." He grinned.

###

Vince's palms started to sweat. Had this girl just said yes to his non-date? He couldn't remember the last time a girl had agreed to do anything with him that wasn't a class requirement.

"Where do you want to go? The next act is about to start." Gaby pointed to the jazz trio setting up on stage.

Think fast. What would be open now? Nothing outside—too cold. No way would he invite a girl back to his dorm room. It was a mess and smelled like his roommate's leftover pizza from a few days ago. "How about the music school?"

"Sounds cool," she nodded. "I've never been there before."

"Most people haven't. We music majors are an insular breed."

She laughed again. "And you're going to let a non-music major into your secret club?"

Her laugh caused his insides to flip. What had gotten into him?

"You might not be so excited when we get to the practice rooms. They look like jail cells."

Her free hand flew to her hip. "You're telling me I'm headed to some creepy room in a building I've never entered with a guy I've never met before?"

He gulped. Maybe this wasn't such a good idea.

She swatted him playfully on the arm. "Just messing with you. Let's go."

###

Gaby let out a breath as she pulled up to the old-fashioned brick building. She'd passed it every day on her way to the psychology department but had never set foot inside. She'd figured it was full of stodgy, uptight, classical musicians. Was she crazy to meet Vince here? She pulled into an empty parking spot, then shot a text to her roommate. "At the music school with a new guy." Best to let someone else know her whereabouts, to be safe.

Vince drove up beside her and climbed out of his car. "Hey."

"Hi." She grabbed her guitar from the back seat and moved next to him. "This building looks like a time capsule from the 19th-century."

He chuckled. "That's probably because it is. I don't think they've renovated it much since then. The big bucks go to the science building."

"That's for sure." She glanced at the impressive, modern edifice across the bridge, gleaming with light.

Once Inside, the two climbed up a flight of winding stairs, then stepped into a large hallway lined with multiple metal doors.

She frowned. "You weren't kidding about the jail cell thing."

"Nope." He glanced around. "There aren't nearly as many people here tonight as usual since they're on dates for Valentine's Day. We could probably avoid the practice rooms and jam here if you prefer." He pointed to a couple of lumpy green couches at the entrance to the hallway.

"Sure." *Thoughtful.* He didn't want to shove her into a tiny space with him. She squatted down to pull out her guitar while he retrieved his viola. "So, what do you wanna play?"

"Lizards in the Land, of course." His green eyes twinkled.

"How do you know the notes? You've only heard it once in your life."

He leaned back against the sofa, stretching his long legs in front of him. "I started to play music when I was three using an auditory-first method. I didn't read notes until years later. So I can play by ear."

"You'll play what I sing?" This was incredulous.

"No, I'll improvise."

How in the world could this guy make up something for a song she'd written only a week ago?

"All right." She shifted on the couch. "Might as well give it a go."

She strummed a few chords, waiting for his entrance. Did he even know what key she was playing? Sure enough, just in time for the vocals, he entered in perfect pitch with a low G. He held it for several bars, then moved to D, and back to G. Whoa. Not what she expected. This guy wasn't half bad.

At the start of the second verse, his fingers quickened as he played several faster notes. What an incredible skill, to come up with all this in the moment.

She'd spent hours perfecting this song. When the chorus returned, his eyes met hers. Heat spread to her cheeks as his gaze fell to her mouth. Did he want to kiss her? She didn't even know the guy. But a little part of her wished he would.

His bow moved in perfect unison with the lyrics, but the rich tone of the notes he played was much lower—deeper, like dark chocolate. The two parts blended in perfect harmony.

The song drew to a close, but she couldn't take her eyes off his. "That was incredible," she blurted. "I've never heard anyone jump in like that before, especially not for one of my songs."

"You're brilliant." He beamed as he lowered the viola to his side. "Your lyrics are original, not like the sappy stuff you hear on pop radio."

Finally, someone who understood her.

"You should perform again. When's your next gig?"

Her gaze fell to her shoes. "No idea. I doubt Café Chocolat will have me back anytime soon. I cleared out the place. The moment they see my name, they'll nix my slot."

"Don't write your name. What if we signed up together?"

"Under yours?"

"No. Like a band name."

"Still, they'd all leave again."

"Not if I bring my friends. They'd love you." His face turned red. "They're all gamers who don't get out much and would totally dig your style."

"Do you really think so?"

His lips curved up. "Positive."

"What should we pick for our band name."

"How about No Strings Attached?"

Genius. "Perfect for a string duo." She tapped her guitar case.

"Awesome, I'll sign up for next week."

She planted a kiss on his cheek. "Great. It's a date."

Brass at the Beach

A Spring Break Story

Part 1

Thank goodness the flight was over. Etta let out the breath she'd held for the last several hours. Too much turbulence.

The orchestra director, Mr. Vatchev, a wiry man with toothpick arms, had recruited several Belton University orchestra students to load the last of the suitcases onto the rental bus. He motioned to the rest of them. "Pile in."

With an extra shove, Etta pushed her enormous tuba case into the overhead compartment and scooted next to Brooke, who held an oboe case in her lap. Woodwind players had it so easy compared to the brass.

Etta glanced out the window at the palm trees. What a contrast to the Midwest. She still couldn't believe the Belton University Orchestra had been invited to Guadeloupe to perform for their Maritime Composers Festival.

"I can't wait to hit the beach." Brooke tossed her wavy brunette hair. "I need to buy a new swimsuit while we're here. The one I have is *so* last season."

"How about a bikini?" One of the French horn students, Terrence, laughed from the seat behind.

"Where's your Speedo?" Brooke pursed her lips.

Terrence grunted. "Good point."

Etta's shoulders drooped. No one ever asked to see a tuba player in a bikini. Just skinny woodwind players. Not that she'd be caught dead in one, anyway. But she'd like guys to notice her.

She stole a glance at Terrence, who'd leaned back in his seat and was fiddling with his phone. He never looked her way when Brooke was around.

Half an hour later, they pulled up to a swanky seaside resort. Etta gasped. Compared to the cheap motels where she'd spent family vacations, this building resembled a palace. Palm trees danced in the breeze, while huge columns stood sentinel nearby. The smell of citrus fruits wafted through the air. She breathed deeply to take it all in. How different from the tree-less plains back home.

"Très belle." Brooke smiled. "So luxurious."

The silky way Brooke spoke French sounded exotic. Etta would love her friend's talent with foreign languages. Face it. She was lucky to have passed freshman English.

A bellman in a crisp navy suit with gold trim helped Mr. Vatchev load the suitcases and instruments onto carts. Wow, his dark skin and ebony eyes made her suck in a breath. As one of the few black students in the orchestra, it was nice to see someone else who shared her race.

"Bienvenue à Guadeloupe."

Etta glanced at Brooke for a translation.

"Welcome to Guadeloupe," Brooke said.

The man's face lit up. "*Mademoiselle parle français?* You speak French?"

"Oui, bien sûr. Yes, of course." Brooke batted her long eyelashes.

Oh no. He'd fall for Brooke for sure. This could take a while. Might as well head inside to the lobby.

A giant waterfall cascaded over rocks into a small basin in the center of the room. Plush couches beckoned. When Etta sat down, she gazed at the elegant chandelier suspended from the ceiling.

Moments later, footsteps pounded the marble floors.

"We're checked in." Mr. Vatchev started to pass out key cards. "Everyone's on the seventh floor." His brows furrowed. "No crazy shenanigans tonight. Our concert's only days away, and we need to rehearse."

"Wouldn't *dream* of it." Brooke grabbed her key and turned to Etta. "Let's go, roomie."

###

The next morning, Terrence pulled a new island shirt over his head, careful not to knock his glasses askew. He was practically blind without them. What a rough night. He'd spent half an hour cleaning up after his dumb roommate puked all over the bathroom floor. Why were his fellow brass buddies such idiots? Didn't they know when to turn down another beer? But no, leave it to him—the responsible, scrawny, nerdy one of the group—

to babysit them. He groaned as he hoisted up his French horn case, clicked open the door, and headed down the hall to the elevators.

"Good morning, Terrence. Going down?" Brooke waved from inside the cramped elevator space.

"Morning, ladies." He managed a weak smile as he squeezed between the girls. How could Brooke be so chipper this morning? And still look good? She'd drunk as many beers as his roommate last night.

Clank.

"Whoa, what just hit me?" He rubbed the side of his head.

Etta moaned. "Sorry. This tuba takes up half the elevator."

"That's why you should play French horn." He held up his instrument, which bumped Brooke's oboe case.

"Watch it." Brooke clutched the instrument to her chest. "I just bought this a couple of months ago."

"Sorry," he mumbled.

Brooke's free hand flew to her hip. "You should be. It wasn't cheap."

"I meant sorry you bought the wrong instrument. French horns take the cake."

Brooke rolled her eyes. "Not a chance."

###

The orchestra members filed into the banquet hall and took their seats in a semi-circle surrounding Mr. Vatchev. Etta plopped herself into her usual place at the rear, where no one in the audience would ever see her. Even the other brass players seldom took notice.

When Mr. Vatchev rapped on the podium, silence rippled over the sea of musicians. "Glad you all managed to make it this morning." He glared at the brass section where one of the trombonists sat with a pail next to him.

"Not sure why we had to be here so early," a trumpeter muttered.

Etta agreed, still battling fatigue from trailing Brooke around the night before. Exhausting.

Mr. Vatchev frowned. "Time to rehearse. We shall run through one of my favorite turn-of-the-twentieth-century works, Debussy's *La Mer*.

"What does that mean?" a flutist asked.

Brooke raised her chin. "It means *the sea* in French."

Mr. Vatchev nodded his head in assent. "Yes. Which is where we'll visit after this rehearsal."

The muscles in Etta's stomach clenched. She'd never been to the ocean before. So deep and vast. And on top of that, she'd never learned to swim. How would she handle *la mer*?

Part 2

Gray clouds hung heavy in the air, and a light mist shrouded the resort, as Terrence joined the procession of Belton students on the winding cobblestone path en route to the resort's visitor center. The effects of the coffee he'd grabbed from the hotel café after rehearsal were kicking in. He needed the extra burst of energy on this dreary day.

Mr. Vatchev folded his arms. "I'd hoped for better weather for our excursion."

"Would they cancel?" Terrence squinted at the sky.

The orchestra director shook his head. "No, only if there's lightning."

Brooke stepped up next to them, wrapping her coverup around her. That thin piece of material didn't cover much. Terrence blinked his eyes to avoid ogling.

"We have to swim in this weather? But it's cold." Her bottom lip protruded.

"It's not that cold." Etta traced her hand along a leafy shrub. "Nothing compared to Midwestern winters."

"Good point," Brooke said. "I'll take this over snow any day."

Terrence's insides tightened. "I hope the storm isn't too strong while we're out there."

At the visitor center, Mr. Vatchev presented several tickets to the clerk. She smiled and ushered them into an adjacent room where pictures of aquatic life hung on every wall. Stingrays, turtles, dolphins, whales, and fish peered at him from their frames.

The guide, a young guy maybe in his twenties, grabbed a microphone and rattled off something in French.

This'd be a dull tour if Terrence couldn't understand anything. He turned to Brooke for a translation, but at that moment the guide switched to English.

"Hello, ladies and gentlemen," he said in a thick French accent. "My name is Matthieu, and I'll be your guide. Today, we'll take you on a boat ride to visit the city of stingrays, where you'll have the chance to swim with these exotic sea creatures."

"Ooooh, sounds fun." Brooke stood on tiptoe and peered at Matthieu. "And he's so cute." She giggled. "I love the French accent."

Terrence grimaced. Of course she did. Exotic, Francophile Brooke would never take notice of a colorless, geeky guy like him.

Matthieu ushered everyone outside. Terrence breathed in the scent of the ocean. A long, bright-colored tourist vessel floated in the dock in front of them.

"As you see, our boat is quite the beauty." The guide extended his hand to help the girls board. Brooke accepted it with a smile, then leapt to the deck. Etta, on the other hand, clutched the guide's hand as if her life depended on it. Her face drained of color as she stumbled onto the boat.

Terrence climbed on board, then sidled up next to her. "Etta, are you all right?"

"I'm fine." She blinked several times. "Trying to keep my contacts from popping out. The spray of saltwater stings my eyes. And I'm not used to the ocean."

Those deep brown eyes. And her bright yellow dress suited her dark complexion. Why hadn't he noticed before? Heat rose to his cheeks. Probably just the sun.

Brooke frowned at her friend. "Since when don't you like water? I thought you loved our lake excursions."

"That's different. The ocean is unpredictable." Etta wrung her hands in front of her. "I don't want to think of what lurks in there. Besides, I've never been a good swimmer."

"Sounds like you've watched *Jaws* one too many times." Terrence clapped her on the back. "You'll be fine. Don't worry."

After all the passengers had boarded, the guide closed the entrance gate. They pulled out of the dock with such a lurch that Etta grabbed Terrence's arm for support. Poor girl was scared to death. The light pressure of her fingers sent an unexpected tingle up his arm.

As the vessel left the harbor and sailed into the open sea, Brooke leaned against the railing, a vision in her navy suit with the wind whipping her hair behind her like a sail.

"Get away from the side of the boat, Brooke." Fear laced Etta's voice. "It's not safe to stand that near the edge."

"I'm fine. That's why there's a railing." Brooke ran her hand along the metal bars.

"It's not very high." Etta said, tight-lipped. "You'll topple over."

"Loosen up, Etta." Brooke said.

The wind's intensity increased as they traveled farther and farther out to sea. Like the symphony they'd played that morning, the boat rose and fell in rhythm with the waves. As they sat on deck, a queasy knot formed in the pit of Terrence's stomach. He shivered. Did they expect anyone to swim in this?

Several minutes later, Matthieu resumed his position at the front of the deck while the boat slowed to a stop. "We've reached our destination," he announced. "The captain instructed me to warn you that the waves are stronger than usual today, so use caution as you descend the ladder to visit the stingrays. Please grab your lifejackets and snorkel gear. I'll go first so I can assist you."

Brooke hurried after him, lifejacket fastened tight, and several other students followed suit. As Terrence made his way to the ladder, he turned toward Etta, who shook her head. "I'm not going."

Terrence hesitated. "You sure?"

Etta's hand flew to her mouth with a jerk. "Positive."

"Do you want me to stay with you? I shouldn't leave you here alone if you're seasick."

"No, I'm fine. Go enjoy the stingrays." She turned away.

He paused, then climbed down the ladder and lowered himself into the water.

A shudder passed through his body as the cold water prickled his skin.

"Terrence, look at this." Brooke bobbed along several feet away next to Matthieu, who held a large triangular creature on the flat portion of his palms. "It tickles." She giggled as she stroked the stingray.

Terrence extended a finger and petted its smooth, velvety skin.

Brook laughed again. "It's sucking on my hand."

Terrence pulled his arm away with a jerk. "Where's its mouth?"

"On the underside." Matthieu lifted a portion of the sea creature to reveal its white belly and tiny mouth.

Terrence traced his finger along the underside. "Does it hurt when it sucks on you?"

"No. It's like a little vacuum." Matthieu pointed at the long tail. "What you need to avoid is its stinger."

Terrence swam back a couple of paces. He'd steer clear of that weapon.

Matthieu chuckled. "Don't worry. These stingrays are used to people."

At that moment, an enormous wave caught them, and Matthieu lost hold of the creature.

"Wow, that was a big one." Brooke clutched onto Matthieu for support. "I—"

An ear-piercing cry echoed above the waves. A flash of yellow tumbled over the side of the boat.

Terrence gasped. *Etta.*

Part 3

The wave crashed over Etta with such violence she could barely keep her head above water, even with the life jacket. She tried to scream, but nothing escaped her lips. Instead, her mouth and eyes burned with salty ocean water. As the waves swirled around her, she clutched her floatation device with a vicelike grip. Would it keep her afloat? Her legs kicked harder than ever before. Her eyes blurred to the point she could barely make out the slim figure who power-crawled toward her.

"Grab this!" the person shouted and flung an extra life jacket her way. She embraced the orange flotation device to steady herself. Moments later, she was gliding through the water toward the boat. When she looked up, Terrence tugged on one of the straps to pull her through the water. His bare back and shoulders told her he'd tossed his own jacket. She gripped it tighter.

When they reached the ladder, Brooke was already clambering on deck. She extended her hand. "Hoist her up here."

Terrence wrapped his arm around Etta's waist. He breathed hard with the extra effort to boost her up. Her own breath caught in her throat. She'd never been this close to him before.

"What happened?" Brooke choked as she pulled Etta on board. "Are you okay?"

Etta nodded, her body still shaking. “I am now. I wasn’t earlier.” She lowered her voice. “To be honest, I felt seasick, so I, uh, hung my head over the side of the boat, just as a huge wave hit. Knocked me overboard. I think I lost my contacts in the water. Good thing I brought a few extra pairs. I was struggling to stay afloat when Terrence tossed me his lifejacket and tugged me to the ladder.”

“I’m glad he found you,” Brooke gasped.

Terrence hoisted himself up the ladder. “Me, too.” He grabbed his towel from the bench and wrapped it around Etta. “My next priority is to teach this girl how to swim.”

Etta jolted back. “What?”

He peeled off his goggles and repositioned his glasses. “I’ve done it a hundred times. Worked at the lake for the past several summers. You’ll be fine. I’m sure you already have good breath control from puffing on that tuba.” He grinned.

###

The next day, after another early morning rehearsal, Terrence and the others followed Matthieu to the wildlife center. The scent of sea creatures mingled with the fragrance of the tropical flora that lined the path. First, they visited the outdoor sea turtle habitat. Pools of various sizes, each filled with several turtles, surrounded the students,.

"These ocean creatures can live over a hundred years." Matthieu pointed to a gargantuan reptile in the pool to his right. "Like this one. He's the oldest at the resort."

"Ooohhh, look at these baby ones." Brooke squealed as she stood by a small pool a few feet away. "They're so cute."

Matthieu walked next to her and scooped one up in his hands. "They were born four days ago. Do you want to hold him?"

"Of course." Brooke held out her hands for the little turtle.

"Me too." Etta squeezed next to them. "They're so tiny compared to Grandpa over there." She cocked her head toward the other pool.

"Yes, they continue to grow for many years." Matthieu rubbed his finger along another baby turtle's shell, then handed it to Etta.

"How adorable." She giggled as she held the baby up to her face.

Terrence couldn't peel his eyes from her. Her face brightened with the tiny creature in hand. A part of him had actually enjoyed his chance to play the hero yesterday, to feel the warmth of Etta's body as she'd clung to him at the ladder… *Whoa, time for a swim. I need to cool off.*

###

An hour later, Etta laughed as Brooke sprinted to the enormous pool in front of them.

"We get to swim with dolphins!" Brooke exclaimed.

Etta shuddered as she eyed the aquatic pool. Did the others expect her to swim with a dolphin? Terrence had insisted she learn. But she needed time to think—to clear her head. She glanced at him, but he was deep in conversation with Mr. Vatchev. Had he even thought about her since yesterday? Would he say anything? Maybe he hadn't felt the same spark she'd experienced.

"Etta, did you hear Matthieu?" Brooke's voice cut in.

"What?" Etta snapped back to attention.

"You're up next to swim with the dolphin." Brooke gave her a light shove toward the pool.

"Right."

Etta's legs trembled as she climbed in next to Matthieu. The cool water sent goosebumps up her arms. The dolphin, Capi, swam several feet away.

"When he comes up to you, grab his flippers to ride on his belly." Matthieu said in his thick French accent. He held out his hands to demonstrate the movement.

"You're kidding." She jerked backward.

No time to think. A second later, Capi splashed next to them. His smooth body and majestic tail made him an impressive sight. Etta grasped the flippers and climbed onto the sleek white skin. With a flash, he took off, swimming on his back with Etta perched on top. How exhilarating! She'd never experienced anything like it. Water droplets wet her face as Capi raced around the pool.

When they returned, Etta slid off into the water.

"*Très bien.*" Matthieu patted Capi on the nose. "Now for the *bisous*."

She frowned. "The what?"

"The *bisous*. The kisses." Matthieu puckered his lips.

"What?" Terrence bulldozed forward, arms folded.

Matthieu slid his hand over Capi's back. "After the swim, Capi always gives his rider a kiss."

The creases in Terrence's face relaxed. "Oh, I see."

Brooke nudged him in the ribs. "You jealous?"

Terrence and Etta locked eyes for a moment. "Maybe," he said.

She hadn't imagined it. Something *had* happened between them yesterday. Her heart pounded faster. When she turned around, she found herself face-to-face with the dolphin. Capi nudged his wet nose against her lips, then flopped back to the water.

"How was it?" Terrence asked.

Etta wiped her lips. “Best kiss I’ve ever had.”
He arched an eyebrow. “Really?”
She held his gaze. What was going on?

Part 4

Back at the hotel room, Etta stood with her swimsuit in hand. Nothing about this suited her—the attire, or the idea of braving the ocean again. She sighed, then pulled it on. Hmm, maybe she'd add her coverup, wide-rim straw hat, and red sandals. Perhaps those would draw attention away from her middle.

She grabbed her beach bag, opened the door, and crashed into Terrence.

He laid his hand on her arm. "Sorry about that."

Her face flushed. "No problem."

They walked side by side to the elevator, through the lobby, and out the door. The ocean's salty scent washed over her on the balmy breeze. As they strolled the narrow path, Etta immersed herself in the beauty of the resort's lush landscape. Palm trees overhead rustled in a lazy island breeze. Gerbera daisies, bright against a broad expanse of lawn, lined the walkway until it disappeared into the sand.

Etta knelt to pull off her sandals. Other students splashed in the water several feet away.

Terrence released his grip on her. "Race you to the beach?"

After a moment's hesitation, she nodded. "You're on." In a flash, she sprinted over the hot sand. She clutched her sun hat with one hand and her beach bag and sandals with the other. Wind ripped through her hair and buzzed in her ears. Wet sand slowed her pace, and water pooled in her footprints. “I won!” she exclaimed, panting.

As she pulled to a stop, Terrence slammed into her, and both sprawled into the water.

She giggled as she pushed him off her. “Why’d you do that?”

He fumbled around in the sand. “Why’d you stop?” His hands continued to pat the ground. “Where are my glasses?”

She jumped up. “You lost them?”

“They fell *somewhere*.” The intensity in his voice increased.

A wave crashed around them, and white foam bubbled at her feet. She shivered.

Moments later, the wave subsided. She picked her way over the remnants of debris left by the tide scanning the beach in vain for any sign of glass or metal.

A few feet away, Terrence crawled on all fours like a dog in search of a buried bone.

“No luck?”

He raised his head in the direction of her voice but didn’t meet her gaze. “What should we do?”

She slipped her hand in his and pulled him to his feet. His fingers curled around hers, which warmed more than her hand.

"You'll have to lead me back to the hotel. What time is it, anyway? Do I have time to visit an eye doctor?"

She shaded her eyes. The sun hung low in the sky.

"I doubt it." This time, it was her turn to guide him along the path back to the hotel. The poor guy was as blind as she was without contacts.

When she stopped in her tracks, he bumped into her again. "You've got to stop doing that, especially now that I'm blind."

"How blind?"

He rubbed his eyes. "Uhhh, pretty bad."

"I mean what's your prescription?"

"I think 20/300. Something abysmal." He ran a hand across his forehead. "Why?"

"Great." With a quick tug, she yanked him forward again.

He stumbled to keep up. "How in the world is that great?"

She pushed the door open and guided him through the lobby. "I have an idea. It's crazy, but worth a shot."

###

Terrence held his breath as Etta helped him into the swivel chair at the hotel desk.

"I hope you know what you're doing." He raked his hand through his hair.

"Trust me." She rushed into the bathroom, then returned moments later with something in her hands. With a plop, she bounced on the bed and spun him to face her.

"What's going on?"

"I'm teaching you how to wear contacts."

"What?" His body turned rigid. "You've got to be kidding. I'll never keep my eyes open. Besides, it can't be good to wear someone else's contacts."

"I agree with you. But we're in a foreign country, we don't have access to an eye doctor, and you can't see a thing. Do you want to spend the rest of the trip blind and miss the concert?"

He slumped lower in the chair. "No. Vatchev would kill me."

"Then it's contacts for you."

"What if they're the wrong prescription? Besides, don't you need them?"

"In ordinary circumstances, I'd never recommend this. But if your eyes are worse than mine, this is better than nothing. Also, I brought a couple of extra pairs. These are new."

"I guess I'll give it a try."

"Great." She bent toward him. The warmth of her skin melted him like chocolate on a hot day. Her cute mouth puckered, probably on autopilot from all those years working on her embouchure, as she leaned over him.

Etta pulled his upper lid with her middle finger and his lower lid with her thumb. With her forefinger she pressed the tiny lens to his eye.

He jerked his head back. "What on earth?"

"Hold still." She pressed him against the chair with her other hand and leaned in again. Now was the time to take her in his arms and kiss her senseless. But the moment her hand approached his eye, his head flinched away.

"Terrence, don't move. I've got to do this."

He grabbed her wrist. "This'll never work. I can't let someone poke me in the eye."

She lowered her arm. "You give up?" Her mouth intoxicated him with her minty breath.

"No." He stroked the inside of her wrist. "That's not what I said. I *do* need to try. Myself."

She pulled her hand away. "You think you can?"

He stood up. "Like you said, I don't have much choice. Now guide me to a mirror so I can figure this out."

"All right." She picked up the contacts and ushered him into the bathroom. "I'll wait for you to finish."

###

"I'm headed to the balcony. Holler if you need me." Etta pulled open the sliding door and stepped outside. She needed fresh air to cool off. What had happened in there? For a moment, she'd thought Terrence might kiss her. Their lips had almost met. But if he couldn't see, maybe he hadn't realized how close they were. Geeky Terrence had managed to weasel his way into her thoughts.

As she waited on the balcony, the scents of saltwater and seafood mingled in the breeze. The horizon resembled a canvas filled with brushstrokes and sunset pastels. The water glistened. Light blue became turquoise and darkened to midnight on the far sea. For a moment, the exquisite beauty of the setting drove all other thoughts from her mind.

What would it be like to live this near the sea? She'd spent her entire life in the Midwest, far from the ocean. This was another world. How she wanted to brave her fears and swim in these waters.

A touch on her arm drew her back to the present. When she spun around, Terrence stood nose-to-nose with her, just like the dolphin a few hours before. Either the sharpness of his features without the glasses or the intensity of his gaze caused her breath to catch in her throat. She swallowed. "Do you need more help?"

"Perhaps." A quirky smile played at the corner of his lips.

"I'll take a look." She cradled the back of his head with her hands and examined his eyes.

He reached out to brush her cheek. "Not that kind of help."

A ripple of excitement flooded her body at his touch.

The hotel door clicked, and the two jumped apart.

Brooke dropped her beach bag on the bed and arched an eyebrow. "What are you guys doing on the balcony?"

Etta wiped her forehead. "Well… umm…"

"I dropped my glasses in the ocean." Terrence rubbed his eyes again.

Brooke gaped at him. "That's awful! What are you gonna do?"

"Etta taught me how to wear contacts."

Brooke's eyes grew as wide as seashells. "I thought there was something different about you. Nice."

"Yeah, my vision's a lot clearer now." He winked at Etta.

Electricity pulsed through her veins. "Glad I could help."

Part 5

The night of the symphony concert, Etta and Brooke bustled around their hotel room. Brooke donned a floral sundress while Etta slipped into a golden dress she'd purchased from the gift shop. First time she hadn't worn black to a concert in ages. Would Terrence notice?

"I can't wait for the international buffet," Brooke said. "I hope they serve lobster."

"Ick!" Etta wrinkled her nose. "That sounds awful."

Brooke frowned. "You've never tried it. How do you know?"

"Those creepy creatures that stare at you from the plate? No thank you."

"I'll bet the desserts are to die for." Brooke grabbed her oboe case.

"That's the best part." Etta beamed. "They might have French *mousse au chocolat* or whatever you call it."

"Not the *best* part." Brooke flashed a knowing smile. "There might be a cute French horn player, too."

Etta's stomach flip-flopped. Of course, Brooke would have realized something was up.

When they reached the patio, the knot in Etta's belly unclenched. Twinkle lights hung from trees and the expansive gazebo set up for the orchestra. Illuminated by the pulse of underwater blue lights, the outdoor pool resembled a deep-sea world. A beautiful arrangement of tropical flowers adorned each white patio table. Fresh seafood, blackened under garlic butter with a hint of sage, mingled with the salty air of the beach. The retro music of the Beach Boys blasted through the sound system.

"Don't you ladies look stunning?" Matthieu smiled. The guide sported a fluorescent orange shirt and floral shorts. He extended his elbow. "May I have the privilege of escorting *la belle dame*, the pretty lady, to the party?"

Brooke beamed. "Of course." She looped her arm in his, and they strolled toward the buffet together.

"Nice evening, isn't it?" Terrence's voice filled the night air.

Etta's heartbeat quickened as she pivoted to face him. "Yes, it's a lovely night."

A vibrant-colored island shirt hung low over his khaki shorts. Stripped of his glasses, he seemed different. Or their relationship was different.

His blue eyes bore into hers. "You look beautiful."

Warmth spread to her face. "Thanks. You're not half bad yourself."

He reached for her hand. "What do you say we—"

"Etta," Brooke called as she turned back toward them. "You must check out the buffet. You, too, Terrence. It's to die for."

His fingers tightened around Etta's. "Sounds great."

###

Terrence's mouth watered as he surveyed the spread. The buffet boasted food from all around the world—Brazilian steak, Mexican tacos, chicken piccata, Italian Fettuccine Alfredo, stuffed mushrooms, and bacon-wrapped asparagus. The seafood table was laden with cocktail shrimp, honey-glazed salmon, mahi-mahi, crab bisque, and lobster tails.

He handed Etta a plate. "Hard to decide with so many choices."

She popped a shrimp into her mouth. "Want one?"

"Sure."

She held up the shrimp and offered a bite. The garlic butter melted in his mouth. His brain turned fuzzy at her proximity. "Delicious."

"Come join us!" Brooke called from a nearby table where she sat with Matthieu.

Normally, he'd have jumped at the chance to sit with Brooke. But tonight, Terrence only had eyes for Etta.

With a little tug on his hand, Etta pulled him along and they sat down at Brooke's table.

"Which dish do you like best?" Brooke forked a piece of fish into her mouth. "I thought I'd pick the lobster, but now I'd vote for the mahi-mahi."

"I'm partial to salmon." Matthieu raised a bite to his mouth.

Terrence eyed Etta, who spread tuna over a slice of bread. "I'd say *tuba* fish."

Her cheeks turned as red as the lobster on her plate.

###

After Terrence had stuffed himself like a crab, he and the other musicians congregated in the gazebo for the concert. Mr. Vatchev had selected the top players of the Belton Symphony to perform for the Maritime Composers Festival. They'd begin with a tribute to the French composer Joseph de Bologne, also known as *Le Chevalier de Saint-George*. A native of Guadeloupe, the eighteenth-century black composer had made a name for himself throughout Europe and the Caribbean. Tonight, the orchestra would perform his *Violin Concerto No. 9, Op. 8* with Belton's violin teacher as the soloist.

Mr. Vatchev raised his arms to lead the opening bars of the violin concerto. Where was Etta? Oh, he'd forgotten. She didn't play the first work. The tuba didn't exist in the eighteenth century. He attempted to focus his eyes on the score in front of him. His vision, while not perfect, was a significant improvement from his usual blind state. He could grow accustomed to this new way of viewing things: the music, the atmosphere, the people, Etta.

###

After the final flourish of the violin soloist's bow, Etta climbed the stairs to her place under the gazebo. How wonderful to finally hear the orchestra perform a piece by a fellow black musician! About time.

A moment later, Terrence caught her eye and looked right at her, through to her soul, as though the contacts painted her in a new light.

Mr. Vatchev nodded to the musicians, and swirls of notes poured from the strings as Debussy's *La Mer* soared into the night air. This trip might change things for her. Maybe she'd shed her cloak of obscurity, at last, and be noticed for who she really was: the girl behind the big brass.

After a half hour of glorious music, the notes died away. Applause erupted from the audience as Mr. Vatchev gestured for the musicians to stand. Etta beamed at her fellow brass players, proud to be a member of such a skilled section.

The orchestra members filed out of the gazebo, and a jazz combo took their place.

As the music started, Etta's foot tapped along to the beat.

Terrence tipped his head at the group. "That's what it means to play brass."

"Yeah." She took a deep breath and allowed the rhythm to pervade her senses.

A small group of people congregated on the dance floor. Matthieu fawned all over Brooke as they danced together.

Terrence traced a finger along Etta's arm. "Should we join them?"

She shook her head. "I don't dance."

"Come on, it'll be fun." He extended his hand to her. "You need to let loose once in a while."

"Oh, all right." She allowed him to pull her up.

His grip tightened around her fingers as he escorted her to the dance floor. Brooke was teaching Matthieu a rousing line dance while the band played a fast song. She waved them over. "Come on, I'll show it to you guys."

After several tries, Etta got the hang of it—clap, hop, repeat in another direction.

Next, the band slowed into Bobby Darrin's classic "Beyond the Sea."

"I need some water," Brooke gasped. "All this dancing makes me thirsty."

Matthieu motioned to the table. "Sit down. I'll grab glasses."

Terrence nudged Etta's arm. "It's stifling here. Let's find a less crowded place." They strolled away toward the beach. Despite the dark night, the sound of the surf crashing on the sand reminded her of the nearness of the ocean.

Terrence turned her to face him. "Wanna dance again?" He slipped his arms around her back.

Words failed her. She nodded, and her hands found their way to the nape of his neck. In his arms, she swayed back and forth to the rhythm of the music and the waves. The peaceful sound of the ocean rang in Etta's ears as she leaned her head against Terrence's cheek. His heartbeat thumped against her chest. He squeezed tighter, expelling the air from her lungs. One hand cradled her neck, and the other pressed tightly against her spine. A moment later, his lips brushed against hers. All fear receded as if with the tide. She surrendered to his kiss. His fingers stroked her hair. He kissed her deeper, as if to explore the depths of the ocean. He wasn't a *French* horn player for nothing.

The fireworks exploding inside her mirrored those bursting over the water that same moment to the fanfare of the brass band. Balls of fire painted the sky in brilliant shades of silver and gold.

When they pulled apart, a sheepish smile graced his features. "Ready for your first swim lesson?"

She gasped. "Now?"

"Sure. Nothing beats a night swim."

"All right." She succumbed as he pulled her toward the water. "Just don't lose your contacts."

"Believe me, I'm never going to lose my sight again." He squeezed her tight as they fell together into the waves.

Return to Mozart

A Winter or Spring Story

Amadeus Gruber lowered his heavy frame into his desk chair. Johann Conservatory wanted him to transfer all of his classes from in-person to online by the end of next week. Would he ever figure out how to navigate the technology? How could they expect this of a sixty-eight-year-old professor? He'd only recently learned how to send photos to his nieces and nephews back in Austria. He needed someone with a better grasp on technology. Perhaps Lisandra, his graduate assistant, could help? Why in the world had the department sent him a female graduate student? Over the course of his career, he'd met very few women interested in composition. Performance, of course, always seemed anxious to show off their fancy dresses at recitals and concerts. But the behind-the-scenes, solitary work of a composer? Not a chance.

He opened his computer, pulled up his email, and began to type.

Dear Lisandra,

Would you be available to help me with my online classes? I am confused by all the new technological requirements.

Best,

Amadeus Gruber

Yes, maybe she'd know more about this stuff, which would allow him to focus on more important things, such as finishing his symphony. After rummaging in the top desk drawer, he pulled out several pieces of staff paper covered in music notes, along with a pencil. He coughed. Again. This blasted cold wouldn't let up. Where had he left off last time? Ah yes, time to add parts for the brass and percussion. Perhaps, with luck, he could begin the developmental section in a couple of weeks. If only this tightness in his chest would ease up.

###

Lisandra's phone rang. Dad. This could only mean one thing. "Hello, Dad, how are you?"

"Honey, you must come home. I'm worried. The airlines are still allowing repatriation passengers on flights, but I'm afraid that soon everyone will shut their borders completely. Please get on a flight before it's too late."

She closed her eyes. "Dad, I can't. Not yet. I still have another two years of school to complete before I finish my graduate degree. And I'm finally getting to study with Amadeus Gruber, a descendent of Mozart himself. You don't expect me to throw it all away, do you?"

"No, dear. But everyone's worried about this virus. They've already canceled all of our symphony concerts for the foreseeable future."

She gasped. "Did you lose your job?"

Silence. "Not yet. But if concert halls don't reopen soon, it might come to that."

Her heart sank. What a devastating blow to her father. He'd worked his entire career to earn his prestigious position as conductor of the Estonian Philharmonic Orchestra.

"Trust me, Dad, I don't like this situation any more than you do. But school is still continuing online, and I've got to pay rent here in New York City. I can't give all this up. Not yet."

"Just think about it." Dad ended the call.

A half-hour later, Lisandra pulled on her fur-trimmed boots and bundled up in a hat, scarf, coat, and gloves. Should she reconsider flying home? What if things grew worse and she couldn't return to Estonia? Outside, a chill stole through her body. She pulled her coat more tightly around herself The eerie empty streets reminded her of old photographs she'd seen from the war. Except this wasn't wartime. But everything was closed, even her favorite café. Would any of these businesses survive? What about symphonies? Surely Dad wouldn't lose his job, would he?

Thank goodness Professor Gruber didn't live far from the conservatory. Once she arrived, she surveyed the elaborate apartment building in front of her. What a contrast to the iron staircases outside her dingy studio.

Of course, she'd never visited her professor's apartment before. The conservatory strongly discouraged such intimate interaction. Would she be safe? She'd read about his history as quite the womanizer back in his day. But since the school had closed its doors, and none of the cafés were open, what choice did she have? She shivered. Hopefully the old bachelor remained respectful.

After knocking several times, the door creaked open to reveal Professor Gruber in the entryway.

"Come on in." He waved her in. "Can I take your coat?"

"I'll keep it on for now. I'm frozen after the walk here."

The sparsely decorated living room begged for a feminine touch, and a glance toward the kitchen showed a mountain of dishes piled in the sink. *Gross.*

Once in his study, he gestured for Lisandra to sit at his computer. "Here you go. I need all the files in the folder labeled 'teaching' uploaded to the new school platform. I forwarded the email with the instructions." He picked up a stack of papers and a pencil. "I'll be in the living room if you have any questions. If not, I'd prefer not to be disturbed."

She nodded.

After a few minutes, she'd located several of the teaching files and uploaded them to his online courses. He'd have benefited from a personal secretary years ago to help with this mess of files.

A couple of hours later, she reread the email from the department to make sure she'd completed everything.

In addition to the files, he'd need to record several lectures and upload them. No doubt he'd need help with that, too. She grabbed her purse and entered the living room. "Professor Gruber, do you need anything else today?"

He shuffled several papers around without looking up. "No, Lisandra. That'll be all for today."

She cleared her throat. "The email mentioned that you'll need to record your lectures for the classes. Would you like some assistance?"

His head popped up. "Record lectures? Ah, I remember. Yes, I'll definitely need help." He coughed into his hand. "I have no idea how to record videos. Do you?"

"Yes."

"Good. I'll see you soon."

###

Two days later, Amadeus pulled on his best blazer, a button-down shirt, tie, and a pair of khaki pants. Apparently, he needed to look professional for the video recording. No use for his students to see him in the sweats and loafers he'd worn for the past twenty-four hours. If only these body aches would ease up so he could accomplish something productive.

He glanced at his watch: 8:15. Time to check his glucose levels. *Hmm, 160, a little high.* All this monitoring of his diabetes would kill him.

A faint knock at the door greeted him.

He attempted a smile and opened the door. "Welcome, Lisandra." His eyes narrowed at the blue medical mask that covered her face. "What's that for?"

"The governor recommended we all wear them. They're supposed to slow the spread of the virus."

He crossed his arms. "Seems a little odd that I can't see your face, but all right. Let's get started. I've prepared my lecture."

"Great." She set up a tripod and mounted her smartphone on top.

"Nice contraption you have there."

She smiled. "Thanks."

Forty-five minutes later, he finished his speech on the rules of harmonic progressions. Palms sweaty, he wiped them on his pants. Must've been the nerves of speaking in front of the camera. "How did I do?"

"Great, Professor. Just like in class." Her eyes shone with enthusiasm. Quite the beauty.

He loosened his tie. "Felt a little odd talking to a camera instead of a room full of people."

"I'm sure you'll get used to it." She turned and picked up a stack of papers from his table. "May I ask what these are for?"

His insides churned. "Be careful. That's the manuscript of my symphony. I've been writing it for several years now, but I haven't had enough time to devote to it. Until recently, of course, now that we can't go anywhere." He grunted.

Her brown eyes scanned the pages as if to take them all in at once. "You know, I could help you input all this into a music software system. That way you could change parts as needed and not have to do it all by hand."

"Hmmm." He stroked his chin. "I've always wanted to try one of those but never had the nerve to take the plunge. I'm so technologically behind that I'm not sure I could figure it out."

She set the stack back on the table. "No worries. I'll help you. It would be my pleasure. I don't have anything going on right now, anyway."

"Excellent. See you tomorrow." With an assistant, maybe he could make faster progress on the composition, if his body cooperated.

###

That evening, Lisandra hurried to the keyboard in her apartment. Would she be able to play the melody to Professor Gruber's symphony? She'd only scanned it for a few minutes, but based on the part she saw, she couldn't deny this man was a musical genius, as evidenced by his eccentricity. The melody had played in her head the whole walk home. If he'd let her help him, maybe now she'd have a chance to prove herself. The need to compose burned in her like a raging fire.

The next morning, she returned to his apartment, her small keyboard in tow. "I'm ready."

"Good." He coughed several times. "Let's get started."

Was he sick? What if he'd contracted the virus She pulled her mask more securely over her face.

With a swift motion, he handed her five stacks of paper. "These are the string parts for the first movement. Once you've finished them, we can move on to the winds. I'm still working on the brass and percussion but will hopefully complete those soon so I can move onto the slow second movement. I think something much more melancholy than the first."

"Makes sense to me." Heart drumming fast, she examined every detail of his composition. The mastery with which he wove the melody from instrument to instrument while adding harmonic layers above and beneath sent a tingling sensation down to the tips of her toes. "This is brilliant," she exclaimed as she ran her fingers over the keyboard. "You're brilliant."

His eyes softened a few degrees as he scrutinized her face. "Thanks. Now tell me, do you have any ideas for the melodic motif of the second movement? Nothing has struck me yet, so I've moved on to the third instead." He coughed into his hand.

"I, um…" Why couldn't she think of anything off the top of her head? "I'll brainstorm tonight and see if I come up with something by tomorrow."

"Perfect." He coughed again. "I'll see you then."

That evening, Lisandra pondered endless musical possibilities for the second movement. Which one should she choose? What would he like best? After two hours, she grabbed her phone. Time for a mental break. She scrolled through several stories about additional businesses that had closed for good. Of all the years to live in New York, this was the absolute worst. With her studies in the fall and her return home to Estonia over the winter break, she'd had little chance to visit any of the sites before everything shut down. Would the world ever return to normal?

###

A week later, Amadeus tried to take a deep breath as he pulled a polo shirt over his head. He shuddered. The body aches and cough hadn't diminished. They'd increased, and now a nasty fever plagued him as well. No use denying the symptoms anymore. Better warn Lisandra. He'd grown accustomed to her presence over the past few weeks—the one ray of light in his isolated, pain-filled days. She was young but smart. The complexity of her suggestions for the second movement blew him away. Not something he'd ever expected of a woman. He'd had many girlfriends in his early years, but no one who truly understood his work. But this girl was different. Her talent and determination signified the ability to become one of the greats.

Yes, he must warn Lisandra. Hopefully it wasn't too late.

###

Lisandra set her phone down on the couch. Now Professor Gruber had the virus. Everyone she knew had fallen sick with this awful virus. It had already killed so many people in New York, and many more were dying by the day. While scrolling her phone again, a disturbing headline caught her eye. "Hundreds of Bodies Buried in Unmarked Graves in New York." Her eyes bulged. This couldn't be true. She continued to read the article. "As numbers in the city skyrocket, overwhelmed authorities, unable to keep up with the body count, have transported many of the unidentified deceased to Hart Island to be buried in mass, unmarked graves."

A sob caught in Lisandra's throat. How inhumane, like something from a page in history. Hadn't she just read a biography about Mozart which referenced his unmarked grave? She closed her eyes at the thought of his dug-up grave, used again and again. This concept of unmarked graves, and mass graves, was a thing of history, wasn't it? How could these exist now, in the twenty-first century, right here in New York City? Like living in a gothic novel.

She pulled out the biography and skimmed the relevant chapter. "Many poor people were buried in pits, or *grubers* in German."

Grubers? Like the last name of her professor? His last name meant "pit?" She shuddered.

The following day, no call from Professor Gruber. Or the next. Or the next. She'd called him but he hadn't answered. Should she risk a visit? His family lived in Austria, while hers was back in Estonia. What if no one had checked on him?

Yes, she had to go. It was the only humane thing to do.

Upon arrival, she rapped on the door several times. Silence. Since he'd given her a key, she turned the latch and stepped inside. The putrid scent of days-old food and dishes assaulted her senses. *Please let him be alive.* What would she do if he wasn't? Her stomach lurched at the thought. *You can do this, Lisandra. Be brave.* She padded to his bedroom door, took a deep breath, and knocked.

"Who's there?" a weak voice croaked.

Thank goodness he wasn't dead.

"It's me, Lisandra. I've come to check on you."

He coughed several times, low and guttural. "Go away. I'm very sick and don't want to risk your exposure."

She hesitated. How could she leave him in this condition alone and to become the next composer buried in an unmarked grave? No, she had to help.

With a deliberate push, she shoved open the door and stepped inside. The professor lay on the bed, his shirt drenched with sweat, face flushed. She brushed her hand against his forehead. Too warm. "How long have you been like this?"

He shrugged. "I don't know. Several days."

"When did you last eat something?"

"Yesterday morning or the day before. I can't remember." He clutched his chest.

She scraped her hand through her hair. What if she'd come a day later? Who knew what might have happened? "We've got to take you to the hospital."

He shook his head. "I can't. According to the news on TV, they don't have enough beds left. Might as well save them for those who have a chance."

Lisandra grabbed the empty cup from his nightstand, filled it with water, and brought it back. "Here, drink this."

With a weak smile, he raised the glass to his lips. "Thank you."

"What else do you need? I can make eggs, if you'd like."

"No."

"You have to eat or you'll lose all strength."

"No."

She wrung her hands. "What do you want to do?"

"Bring me my composition. I want to work on the symphony."

"Not unless you eat first."

His eyes narrowed as he examined her. "You're a stubborn girl, Lisandra. All right, I'll take some eggs if you promise to help me with the symphony afterward."

She smiled. "I promise."

###

Amadeus kept his eyes on Lisandra as they ate their scrambled eggs, canned fruit, and stale cookies. Resourceful. She'd made the most of what remained in the pantry. Perhaps now he'd have the strength to compose. He rose to move to his study, but a pain in his side forced him back in bed.

"Stop." She pressed his hand. "I'll bring the keyboard in here."

When she returned, she sat on the bench and began to play.

"What's that?" he asked after several moments.

"A tune I made up."

"That's it. The theme for the second movement. It's perfect."

Her eyes lit up. "You think so?"

He nodded. “I’d orchestrate it by giving the theme first to the winds, then to the strings. Maybe even add the harp.”

“The harp?”

“It’s your primary instrument, is it not?”

She nodded.

“Yes, let’s do that. I wish I could hear you play.”

“I could bring my harp here tomorrow. I have a portable one.”

“No, you shouldn't come back here. I’m too sick and contagious.”

She wiped his forehead. “I’ve already been exposed.”

He closed his eyes. He struggled to breathe. Why was this virus so unrelenting? If there was a God, thank goodness he’d sent this angel to stay by his side.

###

“You cannot stay at that man’s house.” Dad’s voice crackled over the phone.

“Why not?” Lisandra packed more of her clothes into a suitcase.

“For several reasons. First and most important, because he has the virus, and I don’t want you to contract it. Second, because you’re a young girl and he’s your professor. I don’t want him to take advantage of you.”

Lisandra clipped her suitcase shut. “Dad, he’s so weak he couldn’t take advantage of me, even if he wanted to. And if I get sick, as well, I've already taken that risk. I'm young, so I'd have a good chance of fighting it off. But he's old and has no one here to care for him. Haven't you taught me my whole life to help others?"

Silence.

"Please, Dad, I believe I'm called to do this. I need you to understand."

Dad grunted. "I'll try. Keep us posted. I love you."

"I love you, too."

###

The following morning, Lisandra maneuvered her suitcase and harp to the elevator of Professor Gruber's apartment. What a job.

Once inside, she headed straight to the bedroom. She gasped at the sight of Professor Gruber, lying ashen faced on the pillow.

"Lisandra, is that you?" he whispered.

"Yes." She rushed next to his bed. "How are you?"

"I can't get enough air."

She pulled out her phone. "We're going to the hospital."

He shook his head. "It's too late. I won't make it."

Tears stung her eyes. "You have to. We haven't finished the symphony. We still need to write the fourth movement." She reached for the manuscript that lay next to his bed.

He gave her a weak smile. "From the moment I first heard you play, I knew you possessed what it takes to be a great composer. Although I can't finish it, I know you will."

She swallowed. Of course she wanted to compose, but at this cost? To watch her mentor die before her very eyes? Tears streamed down her cheeks.

With a soft caress, he brushed them from her face. "Don't cry for me. My time is over, and now it's yours." He drew a rattled breath. "Continue to work hard, and trust your inner muse. You have something inside that guides you and inspires your creativity. Never let that flame burn out."

Warmth flooded her heart at his words. He, a descendent of Wolfgang Amadeus Mozart himself, believed she possessed the talent to be a great composer, too.

Another of his coughing fits interrupted her thoughts. What could she do? The cup of water on his nightstand might help. She reached for it and held it to his lips. After a few sips, the cough subsided.

"What do you have in the case?" He pointed toward her instrument.

"My harp." She sniffed.

"Play for me, please."

She rose, pulled it out, and returned to the chair beside his bed. “What song would you like?”

“Anything.”

When her grandpa was dying, her mother had played Psalm twenty-three for him. She’d said it possessed the power to comfort the sick.

“Yea, though I walk through the valley of the shadow of death, I will fear no evil: for thou art with me.”

His breathing slowed. “A psalm of David the harpist, the great composer of old.” He closed his eyes. “I remember.”

###

Back in Estonia two years later, Lisandra slid into the seat of the concert hall next to her mother. Her big day had finally arrived. The title of the program read “Return to Mozart" and included Mozart’s *Requiem* in honor of those who’d died during the pandemic. She glanced at the inside of the program. Her vision blurred at the picture of Amadeus Gruber featured next to her own.

A moment later, her father took the stage and bowed to the audience.

“Ladies and Gentlemen, tonight we celebrate the reunion of the Estonian Philharmonic Orchestra after more than a year’s hiatus.” The audience erupted into applause. “To commemorate this special occasion, we will enjoy a special treat. The late Amadeus Gruber began this symphony long before the pandemic wracked our globe, when musicians still performed for packed concerts halls without fear of illness.

"Months before Gruber's death, my daughter, Lisandra, moved to New York to study with him at Johann Conservatory where they collaborated on the composition. Sadly, Gruber died before the piece was complete, leaving her to finish the task in his stead. Lisandra, would you please stand?"

Tears streamed down her cheeks as she rose from her seat. After all the years of hard work, sacrifice, and pain, she'd finally achieved her dream of being featured alongside the greats.

Dad extended his hand toward her. "Without further ado, I present to you the premiere of the *Resilience Symphony*."

Questions for Reflection

A Change in the Winds

1. Do you ever feel that your instrument is overlooked? What can you do to raise awareness for your instrument?
2. Francesca battled nerves regarding her flute solo. How do you handle nerves when you perform? Do you strive for perfection or to do your best?
3. Were you familiar with the composer Antonin Dvorak? Have you listened to his Symphony No. 8? What do you think of the work?
4. Imagine your own ending to Brandon and Francesca's story. Feel free to post a copy to the digital Belton University book club on social media (more information on author's website).

"Bach" from the Grave

1. Have you ever encountered bullying? How did you respond?
2. How can you stand up for others when they're being bullied?
3. Adam and Miguel lost loved ones. Have you ever encountered loss? How did you work through your grief?
4. How do you celebrate October 31-November 1? How does the organ music in this story reflect these holidays?
5. Imagine your own ending to Adam and Miguel's story. Feel free to post a copy to the digital Belton

University book club on social media (more information on author's website).

Get a "Händel" on It

1. Have you ever lost your leadership position to someone else? How did you respond?
2. Sometimes it's difficult to play "second fiddle," but all parts of the orchestra are critical to the music. How do you feel about the role you play in your ensemble?
3. Were you familiar with Handel's *Messiah*? Did you enjoy it?
4. Imagine your own ending to Karen's story. Feel free to post a copy to the digital Belton University book club on social media (more information on author's website).

Christmas Glee Club

1. This story features several Christmas classics. What is your favorite Christmas song?
2. Have you ever had to fill in for a solo at the last minute? How did it go?
3. Do you sacrifice social events for your music? Is it worth it?
4. Imagine your own ending to Sophia and Brett's story. Feel free to post a copy to the digital Belton University book club on social media (more information on author's website).

The Ivory Touch

1. Have you ever played for an important recital or concert? How did you prepare?
2. Were you familiar with the songs in this story? Which did you like best?
3. Trenton specializes in jazz music, whereas Pauline likes classical. What is your favorite musical genre? Do you enjoy a variety of music?
4. How did the pandemic affect your musical endeavors? What did you do to adapt?
5. Pauline's faith helps her navigate the uncertainty of the pandemic. Do you ascribe to a certain faith? If so, how has it helped you cope with the challenges of the pandemic in relation to both your physical and mental health?
6. Trenton believes that love will help carry them through this difficult period of time. Do you agree? Why or why not?
7. Imagine your own ending to Pauline and Trenton's story. Feel free to post a copy to the digital Belton University book club on social media (more information on author's website).

No Strings Attached

1. Gaby's music doesn't follow traditional musical norms. Do you enjoy alternative styles of music? Would you enjoy Gaby's style? Why or why not?
2. At the end of the story, Vince improvises on Gaby's song "Lizards of the Land." Have you tried improvisation? How can you incorporate it into your playing?
3. What do you think of the phrase "No Strings Attached?"
4. Imagine your own ending to Vince and Gaby's story. Feel free to post a copy to the digital Belton University book club on social media (more information on author's website).

Brass at the Beach

1. Etta struggles with self-confidence and self-image. Have you ever battled these issues? How did you overcome them?
2. Terrence originally falls for the Etta's friend, but over the course of the story he realizes Etta's true beauty. Do you look for beauty on the inside of others or simply the outside?
3. Were you familiar with the works by Claude Debussy and Joseph Bologne? Did you enjoy them? Why or why not?
4. Have you ever taken a trip to an exotic location? What was it like?

5. Imagine your own ending to Etta and Terrence's story. Feel free to post a copy to the digital Belton University book club on social media (more information on author's website).

Return to Mozart

1. Have you ever written a song? What was your experience?
2. Historically, women and minority composers have not received a lot of attention. Which ones are you familiar with? How can we encourage more women and minorities to compose?
3. Amadeus Gruber and Lisandra are fictional composers, but several of the others mentioned are not. Are you familiar with the Estonian composer Arvo Pärt? Who is your favorite composer?
4. How did the works and life of Mozart parallel some of the difficulties of the pandemic? Were you surprised by these connections?
5. Did you deal with loss as a result of the pandemic (or another crisis)? How did you work through it?
6. Imagine your own ending to Lisandra's story. Feel free to post a copy to the digital Belton University book club on social media (more information on author's website).

Questions About the Book as a Whole

1. What was your favorite story? Why?
2. Which character did you most identify with? Why?
3. What instrument do you play? Did you like the character who portrayed your instrument? (If your instrument wasn't portrayed, imagine the character who plays an instrument from the same musical family: winds, brass, strings, or percussion.)
4. The characters throughout these stories come from a variety of backgrounds, both musically and other. How do these affect their styles and approach to music? How can you draw from your own background to enhance your music?
5. As an author, I created many of these fictional stories with elements of truth from my own musical experiences. For example, one of my friends did drop his glasses in the ocean on an orchestra trip! Another friend performed a fabulous annual organ Halloween concert. And my Dad's band really did trade instruments to play a prank on their substitute teacher, not that I recommend it. How can you draw from your own musical experience to create a short story, fictional or real? Feel free to post a copy to the digital Belton University book club on social media (more information on author's website).

If you enjoyed this collection, the author would greatly appreciate if you could leave a review on your book retailer's website. This helps others discover the series and allows her to continue writing music fiction.

You can access additional resources created for this series, as well as information about other books by Ashley Rescot on her website at: www.rescotcreative.com (or scan the QR code below).

The Chronicles of Music Majors

ISBN 978-1-7366044-0-3 paperbook
ISBN 978-1-7366044-1-0 eBook
ISBN 978-1-7366044-2-7 audiobook
© 2021 Ashley Rescot

Made in the USA
Monee, IL
28 April 2021